Rites
Sophie Coulombeau

route

First published by Route in 2012
PO Box 167, Pontefract, WF8 4WW
info@route-online.com
www.route-online.com

ISBN: 978-1-901927-52-8

Sophie Coulombeau asserts her moral right to be
identified as the author of this book

A catalogue for this book is available from the British Library

Design:
GOLDEN www.wearegolden.co.uk

Printed and bound by CPI Group (UK) Ltd, Croydon, CR0 4YY

Route is supported by Arts Council England

For Mum and Dad,
and for Harry

Day

When I was fourteen, I did something terrible. At least, that's what some people tell me.

Other people don't think it was so bad. Or they think, at least, that it can be explained. Which apparently makes a bad thing better, in their book.

Occasionally, these two kinds of people will disagree about exactly what happened. That is, there are those hardliners out there who will call one or more of us a liar. But those are the extremists. The vast majority of people, even when they can agree on the what, still fall out over the why and wherefore. They must. They can't help it. Because – this is my own personal theory – these two kinds of people usually hate each other anyway, and they need something to disagree on. My crime is a convenient little litmus test, if you're not yet sure to which kind you belong. You may surprise yourself.

Back when it all happened, what surprised me most was the admiration I inspired. It's terribly funny, you know, what you can get adulated for these days. Do you remember that man, Raoul Moat? He blew a gaggle of innocent bystanders to blazes, then put the gun down his own throat. I can't remember quite why. He had a problem with his mortgage, or thought the window cleaner was squiring his wife, or something along those lines. Well, *he* had fans. And I don't mean apologists, by the way – I mean *fans*. There were hand-wringing editorials in all the broadsheets about how he was the face of the emasculated, jobless, balding and porky underclass. There was a Facebook group set up by some horrid whey-faced female called 'ROUAL MOAT U R A LEGEND' or some similarly poignant moniker. It sometimes appears to me that one can get admired for anything these days. Anything, of course, other than being unremarkable.

I, like Raoul Moat, found support in the most surprising places.

No one really put it like that at the time, of course. There were – alas – no online support groups called 'DAY U R A LEGEND LOL'. Nobody publicly called me the face of the spotty, sexually frustrated, economically underprivileged teenage social substrata, which I would have rather enjoyed if I'm honest. Although this was well before the days of Facebook, or Twitter, or anything else like that, back in that primeval epoch when people wrote letters by hand and email was still considered exotic. So perhaps my fans would have done all this for me if only they'd had the appropriate technology to hand. But, given that they couldn't, they found ways to make their admiration known. For the rest of my adolescence I had a furtive kind of celebrity oozing out of my pores. I could feel it walking into a room, or out of one. A sort of arrested breath. There were the girls who hung around in packs, whispering and digging each other in the ribs and casting me saucy glances. There were the boys who never had time for me before at school, but suddenly started barking *Aright, Brady?* and kicking footballs in my direction like pathetically misplaced talismans of camaraderie. There was the newsagent who started giving me cigarettes for free – even though it was clearer than ever, given what had happened, that I was heinously underage.

I surprised myself, when I left Manchester once upon a time, by missing that feeling. It felt strange to be normal. Cut off cleanly from my history, floating around separately from my crime. Everyone needs some ballast, I think. I came back.

When I was seventeen, my English teacher – who was about to leave the school for a new job – beckoned me over in the pub. He was half-cut and overexcited, and he wore the blunderbuss shine of a man poised upon the precipice of liberation. *Day,* he said, flecks of spit around his lips, *May as well ask it before I go. Did you do it?*

Did I do what, Sir? said I, although I knew immediately what he meant.

Well, did you do it? You know! The thing. The thing, back in the day.

I looked at him. His eyes flickered back and forth, and he stilled a little, and a sort of intensity settled over the group in the pub. I'd never liked him, you see, this man. A buck-toothed weasel with a womanly bottom and an offensively matey facade. He always struck me, for one thing, as one of those who can only get their kicks from the periphery. Proud player of intestine-splattering computer games, who'd never been in a fight. Gold-standard subscriber to pornographic publications that specialise in masturbating up prostitutes' noses, who never got laid. I hate people who, for want of a better description right now, won't get stuck in. But more importantly than any of that, his English lessons were custard-pie tragi-farces of SparkNotes symbols and leaden lectures on 'character'. That was his greatest offence. Anybody who can reduce *Hamlet* to a beginning, middle and end, a wan 'indecisive' or a bleating 'sexist', should be keelhauled and strung up for the condors, not made privy to enterprises of great pith and moment.

I looked at him, and I saw that he *wanted* me to have done it; I saw him projecting himself into my youthful place and thinking of the thrill, the titillation, the exquisite wrongdoing of it. I said, *No, of course I didn't. I said that at the time, didn't I?* And then I did my very best aggrieved. I do a good aggrieved, always have. I have some hard work to put into my humble, and frankly my penitent will never win any prizes, but aggrieved? Never been a problem. Of course, he was duly crestfallen. Ever so embarrassed. Stammered something about a joke and bought me a drink, which I accepted with the grace of a martyr.

He, like so many others, wanted me either to swagger or to

hang my head. But why would I? I wasn't ashamed, or proud. Not really. Not predominantly. I was angry.

I think I'm still angry, you know. You don't get over that sort of thing in a hurry. It's only been fifteen years.

I should probably take the rough with the smooth; accept that if you're going to be someone, then you've got to take a spiky chaser of infamy along with your long and fruity fametini. *Infamous*. That's a funny word, isn't it? For years I used to pronounce it 'in*famous*', as if it were just 'famous' with 'in' affixed on the beginning like a heraldic trumpet blast. The uber-fame! The best, sexiest, most Byronic type of famous. But then some snotty girl once pointed out to me, some years after the incident, that not only did 'in' generally represent an inversion rather than an intensification, and therefore logic would dictate that to be infamous was to be the opposite of famous, but that actually it was pronounced '*in*-fummus', that in fact infamy wasn't much to do with fame at all, lexically speaking. That relationship did not last long. In fact, I think I may have ended up cradling a kebab and remote control that very night, instead of the fragrant Caroline. And to this day, I've tried not to use the word 'infamous' again, unless it be to ponder its incongruousness.

I digress.

There's this little thing called the truth. It *wasn't* just me. The four of us were all in it together. And yet it was me who got the blame. Now, I wonder why that was? Can you think, looking at me, looking at the others, of any possible reason why that might be?

Hold on. I'm being unfair, aren't I? You don't even know me yet. I should tell you some things. About me and us and what happened, and why. Then you can make up your own mind.

How would you like it? In chronological sequence, or the facts in order of importance? As a picaresque narrative or a courtroom drama? A Q&A or apologia? The choice is yours. I can oblige.

I have thought about it, I assure you, in every conceivable format. They all have their advantages, but I'm not sure you're ready for my more outlandish species of narrative. Perhaps it would be best to start you off with a couple of questions. The important things. We can snuffle down into the dirtier details later on. I don't know how long you've got.

Here we go, then.

1. Why did we decide to do it?
2. How did it go so wrong?

Now, I never manage to answer either of these questions to my own satisfaction, not really. But one has to try. There's no point in not trying. My efforts this morning went like this:

1. Because the four of us lived on the same street.

There were other conspirators available, you know. I've often amused myself – if you can call it amusement – by picturing the faces of those other vague, unimportant others whom I might have involved in the plan, and how it might have all been different if I had involved them. But I didn't. So you don't need to know about any of the others. It was us four in the end. And I think, I *think* though I'm not entirely sure, that it was us four in the end simply because we lived on the same street. Geography's important, you know, when you're fourteen years old. You forget, once you're grown up, how *bound* you are when you're that age. I mean, individual circumstances differ, obviously – you'll find that out later. But in general you have none of at least one of the following things: money, time, privacy, autonomy. Your world is what's on your doorstep.

Or at least, it is if you don't have a bicycle. Which I didn't. Because I always found them inexpressibly vulgar. I told Nick as much when he got one, perhaps in rather harsh terms, long before all this stuff happened. He blustered a little, as is his general wont – have you met him yet? You'll see what I mean – but subsequently ceased to parade up and down the Close on it in that ridiculous fashion, earning general pity. He has yet to thank me.

Anyway, I *liked* our neighbourhood. I didn't really want to get out of it. Have you noticed how some streets have a sort of sinister smoothness to them? I like to think that it's born of the fact that everybody on the street is basically the same person. Same income bracket, same taste in décor and garden gnomes, same hilariously hypocritical attitude towards garish Christmas decorations, same dreams and hopes and ambitions, same wearyingly unoriginal ways of dealing with their wearyingly unoriginal miserable marriages. They all think the same about things like pub closing times and litter louts and pedestrian crossings and new flats springing up and causing problems with the parking. They have well-oiled residents' associations, and when there's an election the windows are a spooky sort of cornfield of uniform red or blue or purple or whatever it is.

Well, our street, Chesterton Close, wasn't like that at all.

It was me, Lizzie, Nick and Rachel. Because we all lived on the Close. We weren't anything like a complete circle until that summer though; in many ways, it was the plan and the strength of our will to carry it out that bound us together and gradually pushed out other friends. But there was a shared history. You know the kind of thing. Nick and I had gone to primary school together. We'd all played Sleeping Lions at each others' parties and once Lizzie and Nick had fallen out – blood and tears, I shit thee not – after a nasty game of Musical Chairs. We'd scowled at each other across the church aisles, done First Holy Communion together and taken the same minibus to Confirmation classes. The other three of us had sniggered at Rachel doing the Reading. We'd been farmed over to play with each other when our parents were sick of us. And we'd all done the 11+ and started secondary school together at St Peter's out in Whalley Range. So we all caught the bus together in the morning, from the bus stop just around the corner and caught it home at night.

And when school finished that year and the summer holidays unfolded in front of us, like paper promising wonderful origami shapes if we could only find the right way to fold it, we could be found on the street in the sun and the smell of cut grass and softening tarmac, doing all those things that grown-ups called 'hanging around'. Sitting on walls and talking and laughing too loudly, and bothering passers-by, and eating ice pops from the corner shop.

When I think of Lizzie now – Lizzie as she was before it happened, that is – her lips are always blue. She loved those neon blue ice pops – you know, the ones that make wide-eyed claims to be flavoured with raspberry. She always had trouble opening them. My eternal image of her is sitting there on the wall to Nick's house, chewing and chewing at the plastic flap at the end of the ice pop, with her face scrunched up in frustration. The plastic would become soggy and wormy with teeth marks. And then, always, I'd take pity on her and take it off her. I'd bite the end hard and rip my head away sideways like a dog, and then grin at her with a shred of plastic in my teeth.

It hurt, but I'd never tell her that.

Then I'd hand it back, and she'd look at me and smile, and start sucking out the bright blue juice and making little hissing noises when it chilled her teeth. And gradually her lips would turn blue and her tongue would go a sort of murky pale shade of black.

After it all happened, you'd think she might have made herself scarce. Been ashamed or something. But she seemed to deal with it by being out in the street as much as possible, actually parading up and down the Close on her bike or on foot, walking to and fro around the corner, in front of the flats where I lived, as if to taunt me. Sometimes she'd be by herself, reading a magazine, or listening to music, or just riding or walking up and down. She knew I was watching her. She must have known. I hated her by then.

But I never saw her eat those blue ice pops after it happened. So in my mind they are now equated with innocence, and with our lives before we carried out our plan.

The street. It was because we lived on the same street. And – of course – because it was there to be done.

2. How did it go so wrong?

This one is harder to answer. Here are a few options:
(a) The keys.
(b) The beauty of 5am.
(c) Nick can't take rejection.
(d) Lizzie's an imbecile (See the Sexual Offences Act 1956).
(e) I'm a rapist.
(f) The precise colour of Rachel's cheeks.
(g) The homily.
(h) The grown-ups.
(i) Girls get jealous.

Sometimes, on my bad days, it appears to me as if there was only one way it could have happened, and it ended with all this. It seems that the path of events was traced out long before it first occurred to me to suggest the plan; that it was laid out in invisible ink all those years that we were growing up together, just waiting for adolescence to come along like lemon juice. But I have to constantly remind myself (feeding my anger dutifully) that it didn't *have* to happen that way. If one of those things had been a little bit different…

I suppose that Lizzie should be the natural focus of my anger. But – no. She's just a little dog-eared shape in a thousand-piece jigsaw. A bit of sky behind a church spire, perhaps. The blurred hand of a passer-by. I want bigger targets.

My name, by the way, is Damien Brady. Back then, in the summer of 1997, I was called Day. I was fourteen years old, and I decided one day that it was about time I lost my virginity. That's what you're here to talk about, I presume?

Kathleen

My name's Kathleen O'Leary, and I've lived on this street for twenty-nine years now. It sometimes seems to me like I'm the only one who's been here any length of time. It's all new these days, isn't it? You blink and the shop signs have changed, and what used to be a lovely pub is suddenly a Tesco, or a kebab shop, or something. The change is rarely for the better, if you ask me. Same with people. Soon as they move in, they're packing up to move out. I can't think of another family that's been on this street more than a year or two. All the kids go off to uni – it's all uni nowadays, isn't it? What the heck are they going to do afterwards is what I want to know, when the whole world's got a degree and there's nobody to clean the lavs – and then the parents find the house is too big for them and they pack up to go and grow vegetables somewhere in the country, then the house gets turned into flats for yuppies wanting to be near the Metro stop, or taken over by the council. Well, I'm not going anywhere. I'm staying right here. I've always said that, and I mean it.

I live alone. My husband… well, we're separated. Not divorced, just separated. It's a long story. Look, why d'you want to know all this, anyway?

Some things are best forgotten.

Did Lizzie send you then? Have you seen her?

Why on earth would you care about all that, if she didn't put it in your head? Some trick of hers… It's all best forgotten. I'd really rather not talk about it. It wasn't a surprise, though. I will just say that.

Well, it shames me to say it – you can't imagine what it's like to have to say this sort of thing about your own daughter – but you could've seen it coming miles off. That or something like it.

Look, you. D'you have children of your own? I wouldn't advise it. Especially the girls. If you ever get round to it, pray for a boy. Girls these days are something else, I tell you. When I was young… well, I suppose I grew up in Ireland, it was different in many ways, still might be I suppose… but still! It's a disgrace to see girls these days, over here, anyway. Out at all hours, flashing their knickers, puking in the gutter. Doing God knows what with God knows who in public. Running around with a new boy every week, going behind the cinema and into the bushes with 'em. I was driving down the high street the other day on Friday, it was only eight o'clock or something, when I saw a girl urinating on the pavement next to a skip! Urinating! Girls of fourteen, fifteen years old.

Do you know what makes me angry? It's when people say, *I blame the parents*. Oh, that is unfair. I know myself, from bitter experience, there's only so much parents can do.

You try your best. *I* tried my best. But there was no listening. She always knew better, didn't she.

This'll sound silly to you I imagine, but when she was young she was forever taking her clothes off. All children do, of course – it's normal to a point, people have told me that – but still, there was something… it carried on too long, you know? She was six, seven, eight, and still wanting to run around in the nip. How d'you tell your daughter there's a point where this sort of thing has to stop?

I can pinpoint the first time I knew. Knew there'd be this kind of trouble, that is. She was seven years old. She was playing with one of those boys down the street, I can't remember which one, and I could just hear them in the garden, I was doing something or other in the kitchen but the window was open. I heard her say, *Can I touch it?* And he said, *No, you've already broken yours off*. I found her squatting in the sandpit, in the nip, with her clothes in a puddle next to her, with this little boy with his pants pulled down looking terrified and, like, shielding his thing. I sent him home straightaway, then took her inside and told her to put her clothes on, and sat her down for a talking to. I told her the truth, I said, *Lizzie, the boys will think you're a tramp if you go on like that.* She cried, like she always did when I tried to give her some home truths. It was all for her dad's benefit, really. Paul took her side, of course. He always did. *Don't be too hard on her, Kathleen, she's only little.* Oh yes, very good. Very bloody good, Paul. Look where that got us.

So, when all that stuff happened a few years later, I won't say I wasn't upset. Upset? I was humiliated. I was mortified. But I wasn't surprised.

I don't blame him. Oh, you could tell it wasn't his idea. Silly little eejit. He carried the can because she wouldn't. I don't know. It's a grief and a shame to think about the whole thing.

I haven't seen her for years. You probably know that. Paul told me not to ask for custody, or he'd drag everything out in public. Tell everyone everything. Well, that shows what kind of a man he was, in the end, after everything. *Good riddance then,* I said.

I still love her. Of course I do. She's my daughter. I'm not some kind of monster. I look at her picture every now and then, I still have one in a frame. From when she was a baby.

Sometimes I wonder what she's doing, where she is now. I'm afraid it won't be good news. Some girls are headed for disaster. She's one of them. I can say it, I'm her mother. And a mother knows. I think she still lives with Paul. But then, I don't really know, I just hear things. I haven't seen him much since he left. Don't speak to him at all, now.

He chose her, didn't he? He always did.

Rachel

I'm Rachel. I know who you are. Day told me you'd be coming. Well, he made some cryptic remarks about the exhaustion of constant celebrity and the likelihood that I'd be approached for background colour, so I put two and two together.

You've met Day already then, I imagine? So you know what he's like. I don't need to tell you.

Well, maybe I do need to tell you. Lots of people think he's a wanker. And I suppose, depending on how long you spoke to him, and what kind of mood he was in… well, he's not a wanker. Or he's not *just* a wanker, anyway. He has this idea in his head of how things are, or how things were, and it has to be filtered through him, he can't help it. He's capable of doing amazing things with the truth – creative things, incredible things really, although I know that sounds like I'm just making excuses for him.

Let me put it this way. A few years ago, someone took me to a sort of burlesque show at the Hippodrome. I wasn't too impressed – it was basically glorified tits and ass on roller skates. But there was one act that really struck me. This contortionist. He was a perfectly normal-looking guy, perhaps slightly oddly proportioned – his bottom half was skinnier than his top, though that could have been the tight trousers. But anyway, he had a tennis racquet, just a normal-sized tennis racquet that he'd unstrung so it was just an empty hoop, and his trick was to fit his body through it, limb by limb, dislocating himself as he went. You could see his shoulders click out of place, and his hips roll around out of their sockets. It was otherworldly, it was rather horrible and rather magnificent at the same time. The audience watched through their fingers. But he finally did it, finally managed to squeeze his disjointed pelvis through the hole and whipped it over his legs and then stood there, sweating and triumphant and saying with his body, *I'm still me, but I've come through* that, and the music crashed and the drums rolled and everyone applauded. And I thought of Day. But Day would be the tennis racquet and the body would be the truth. The truth has to fit through *him*.

Look, the point is, he has this version of things, and it's not a lie exactly because he's not conscious of making it up. He *believes* it. He was convinced that I had sort of always grown up with the three of them, for example, that we all had this shared history. Well, that's rubbish. They – Lizzie and Day and Nick – had all lived on the street since they were born, practically, but I was a bit of a latecomer. We didn't actually move to the Close, to England, until I was eleven. Dad got a transfer and we moved. I had to leave my friends in France, oh you know, the same old story, happens all the time. I was the new kid on the block, I was awkward, I was homesick, I was fat and I wore terrible clothes, and Dad thought of all these ridiculous things that he imagined would help me to fit in and make friends. Like doing the Reading. *God.* So, I was a loner for the first three years of my life on Chesterton Close. The other three of them weren't even really friends with me until that summer, when we were fourteen.

In fact – look, this whole thing isn't really about me. But I know I was there, and I suppose I have some measure of responsibility for it. Especially for what happened at the end. Yes, I suppose you could say that how it finished was all because of me. So… if I had to say why I got involved, it would probably have a lot to do with the Reading. And everything that the Reading stood for in my head. That I was uncool and a bit chubby, and that I had to go to mass and embarrass myself in front of everyone to please my dad. I wouldn't say I was *rebelling* exactly. There's too much luggage attached to that word. But this was a way of carving out who I wanted to be. Even if it just involved going along with what somebody said to do, at least it was what *someone other than Dad* said to do. What's more, it was Day.

When I was younger, when Mum was still alive, and if I did something silly like eat berries off a shrub because a friend said to do it, she'd say, *And if so-and-so told you to jump under a bus, would you do it?* Rhetorical question, of course. *No, Mum.*

But the thing is, by the time I was fourteen, Mum had been dead for years. And if Day had told me to jump under a bus, then I think I would have said, *What number?*

Are you religious?

Lots of people round our way were Catholic, you're probably starting to figure that out. Including me, nominally. I'd been baptised, taken my First Holy Communion at seven, been confirmed at twelve. But never in my head. Never. All the time I was growing up, it was just another of those fictions that you can't say are fictions, on pain of death. Like when you pretend that it's not unusual that your next-door neighbour's in a wheelchair; or you pretend that your friend's Uncle Bob isn't creepy. You can't say there's no God, even if you know it's true.

But I'd always hated the mass, always, even when I couldn't say it. I still do. It was stamped through me from day one, like through a stick of rock. I remember crying when I was little, in church, all the time. I mean, what toddler *wouldn't* be frightened? Those icons with their bleeding hearts and their horrid blank eyes. All the chanting and the organ and the heavy silences. *Being judged.* I remember very well, too well, being carried out of a service by Mum, screaming.

It used to ruin my week, you know. Having to go to church. Sundays, entire weekends, always had this horrid shadow cast over them. By Saturday afternoon, I'd be thinking about it. By Saturday evening, I'd be dreading it. And then Sunday, when the hands of the clock creeping around to five o'clock made me feel slightly sick every time I looked at them. I had to change out of play clothes into a dress – I hated wearing dresses, still do actually. Brush my hair so it got all static. Walk to the church with Mum and Dad gripping my hands, and sit for forty-five minutes on a cold pew trying not to breathe in that piss-and-lavender smell of old people. And listening to all the sanctimonious shit they feed you. They sing it in France and they speak it in England, but it's the same shit the world

18

over. I would look around at all the people chanting, standing up, sitting down, kneeling, bowing in unison, and feel utterly disdainful of them and yet afraid of them at the same time. I didn't want to look at my parents in church, ever, in case it made me hate them.

And then, after Mum died, when Dad and I moved to Manchester, to the Close, we started going to the local church and doing all the things in the parish that we'd done in our last home. But in addition to this, as if all this wasn't enough, Dad decided that I should start to do the Reading. It was a shady deal that took place between him and Father Patrick with no consultation of the main party. My name went up on a rota and I'd do the Reading every fourth Sunday, and that was that.

There was this particular Reading – God, I'm getting furious just thinking about it – about the breasts of Jerusalem. I remember it perfectly. Do you want to know how it goes? It goes like this. *Be glad for Jerusalem, all you who love her. Rejoice, for her, all you who mourned her. That you may be suckled, filled, from her consoling breast. That you may savour with delight her glorious breasts.* Yeah. I know. And I always got it! Every single bloody year! It's like it was a conspiracy between all the parish elders: *Oh, I know! Let's make the awkward prepubescent girl do the bit about the breasts of Jerusalem, let's make* her *quaveringly invite the octogenarian congregation to come to them and suckle.* I read it out in a whisper, I felt grubby and miserable and mortified all at once, and burned with hatred for Dad and the mass, for putting me through the ordeal. I could see all the cool kids who sat on the radiators at the back of the church, under the noticeboards, sniggering at me. I tried not to look at Day and Nick and Lizzie because it hurt the most to know they were laughing at me. They were the ones I always wanted to be friends with.

Anyway, my point is that I think I wanted to be a part of it because of always having to do the Reading. I was strung up every fourth Sunday for the others to laugh at, and this was some sort of way for me – though the connection might not be obvious to *you* – of giving them all, Dad and Father Patrick and all of those churchgoing zombies, a massive poke in the eye. Or something worse.

Of course, I couldn't have known what would happen. I think I'm the only person who doesn't blame someone or other for it. Either Day or Lizzie or both. It was crossed wires, that's all. These things happen.

I still speak to Lizzie. I think I'm the only one who does. It took her a long time to forgive *me*, ironically enough. But I got there in the end.

Father Patrick Creevey

I'll tell you what I think of the whole business.

I think that kids will be kids.

It sometimes surprises people that I say that. As if I'm supposed to hail down fire and brimstone on 'em for it. Well, sorry to disappoint. We, the Church, we're a subtler species than many people imagine. Anyway, I'm retired now. My fire and brimstone days, if I ever had them, are over.

Look, some of the things I saw in my time as parish priest… you stop being surprised. Remember, it's part of the job description that people *have to tell you everything they've ever done wrong.* Just think for a moment what that might involve, any given week. We're talking theft, fraud, assault, rape, domestic violence, buggery, betrayal, adultery, incest, blackmail, bestiality. We're talking punching your elderly mother in the face when she won't stop nagging, we're talking fiddling your father's pension to fund your prostitution habit, we're talking cheating on your terminally ill husband with his brother. I've had two murders in my time. One spontaneous, the other premeditated.

So, in comparison, hearing children confess is a bit like being pelted with cotton wool balls.

Sure you've got to advise people about what to do, and the

advice is often heavy on the restraint and repentance and not so heavy on the indulging your every fleshly desire, but you dispense it with a kind of automated quality after a while. It's not personal, you're not *shocked,* like. Well, one of the murders was pretty shocking, but even that – you just get on with the job. Although in one way you're obviously there to judge, in another – well – you're not there to judge. Or people wouldn't come to confession, would they?

Look, I'm one of those who believe that the Church needs to adapt to survive in the modern age. Not that we need to go around okaying abortion and celebrating divorce and all that kind of stuff. But there are certain aces that the Church has up its sleeve that I believe we haven't really made the most of, to date. Like confession. Confession is a fantastically versatile thing, you know. It speaks to an ancient and inherent instinct which is also an extremely modern need. The need to tell all. The need to confess. To purge. To share. Confession is, to be sure, the principal method of making all square between you and God, of cleaning your slate in preparation for death and Judgement Day. But it is also free therapy.

In fact, there is one particular way in which confession as administered by the Church can knock this modern, showy, two-hundred-quid-an-hour therapy into a cocked hat. We don't just listen. We don't just help you to understand yourself. We can forgive. We can tell you what to do, give you a concrete penance, and tell you *You're alright now, you're clean. Go on, here's a fresh start, go out and enjoy it. That's it! You don't need to feel bad about it anymore!* And this is what secular therapy doesn't seem to grasp, or at least hasn't done to date as far as I know. People don't just need to be listened to, and nodded at. They need to be *forgiven.* The burden that's put upon people these days – this idea that *only* you *can forgive yourself* – it's too great a thing to ask of someone. It asks them to be two people at the same time. It's doublethink. Nobody buys it, not really. You know why?

I'll tell you. Because when it comes down to it, everyone's a child at heart. We want a greater authority to forgive us. And the therapists just sit there paring their nails and writing things down on a clipboard. Whereas God can forgive. *I* can forgive, in His name. That's what people really need.

Wouldn't you like to be forgiven for something?

Fair enough! Well, you do seem to be rather occupying the shoes of the confessor rather than the penitent, up to this point. Maybe I'd better be off. Don't want to tread on your toes and all that. Although, like I say, I'm retired. You've got nothing to fear from me, you know. I might just come back and see how you're getting on at some point, if it's all the same to you.

Just remember: they need forgiveness too.

Lizzie

You're talking to everyone else, aren't you? Like, literally everyone else. I've heard you're talking to my mum, even. So, I guess I've not got much choice.

I'm Lizzie. But you probably knew that.

Want a Love Heart? I've got a real sweet tooth, me. Maybe it's because I am basically like a sweet thing. That probably sounds a bit weird, doesn't it? But I'll explain what I mean.

There are two types of girl, right. One of them is like bubble gum – let's say tutti-frutti Hubba Bubba. Have you had it? What I mean by that is, you put it in your mouth and you get this huge burst of exotic taste that nearly overpowers you, you're like *Wow.* Then, as you chew it the taste dies down and becomes dull. It happens quite quickly. And before long, before very long at all, you're thinking that it actually tastes a bit gross and it isn't really worth it. And you spit it out into the bin. That's what I'm like. That's what always happens to me.

Then they go on and eat a Rachel. I haven't figured this bit out yet, I don't know what kind of food she is. But it's the opposite kind of thing. Boys don't look at her twice, you know, at first. I mean, she's thin and stuff these days. But she didn't use to be. That's not really what it's about. When boys spend time with Rachel… she grows on them, like. She doesn't waste all her flavour at the start.

I've tried to change, but it always happens the same way. They can't get enough of me at first. I've tried acting in different ways. Being honest about my feelings, being mysterious, being a bitch, not giving myself away too much, whatever that means. But sooner or later, I give in. I know it's inevitable now. I give in, and then they fuck off. They've had the flavour and suddenly they don't like looking at me anymore, or tasting me anymore, or talking to me anymore, whatever you want to call it. The nicer kind will say something, they'll be like, *it's not you, it's me* or whatever the latest version of that is. But mostly, they just disappear. They just stop texting, they never call again, if they see you they look through you. And I'm alone again. I've always been alone. Apart from my dad.

I actually prefer the kind that abandon you. Means I can hate them.

I see the world in patterns. Rachel says I shouldn't. But you don't choose how you see things. I can only see the same thing happening, again and again. I feel like these days I wouldn't be me without that way of looking at things.

Sweets for my sweet, sugar for my honey. Remember that song? *Oh honey, sugar sugar.* That's another one. *Sweet like chocolate.* There's loads of them, aren't there? Don't know why people make such a big deal about sweets when actually most of them would prefer, I don't know, like, a roast dinner or something.

Day

You know what I could never stand about Lizzie? She says *like* all the time, when she is reporting speech, or trying to express an opinion. *He was like, Oh no,* she'd say. Or, *It's, like, not fair.* Or even, superbly unaware of the irony, *I'm, like, completely sure of it.*

It's as if, when she speaks, she fears complete commitment to anything. She must always have the disclaimer of *like*. As if somebody might come back and hold her to whatever she said.

Nick

Now, how on earth did you hear about that?

I suppose I've told a few people in my time – maybe it gets around. It makes a good story. Not really a pub story – you actually get some funny reactions sometimes if you get the audience wrong. More of a fag-end of a dinner party story, you know, the time of night when everyone's pissed and fondling everyone else's foot under the table.

Or pillow talk. It's surprising how often pillow talk revolves around previous, you know, sex stuff. It's as if people want to place themselves once they've done the deed. Understand where they fit in to the other person's bigger picture. Am I number seventy-nine? Number ten? Number three? (It's never number one these days, unless you make a habit of deflowering minors.) What was the best fuck of your life? What was the worst? And, of course, who was the first. Eventually you always get there, don't you? How old were you, who was it, what happened? And that's when I tell that story.

Told, I mean to say. All that's over now. I'm a married man, as you can see. Christina – that's my wife, Chrissy – she's heard it a few times. I don't think she likes it, actually. She liked it the first time – girls love a bad boy, no matter what they say – but I think she might be a bit sick of it now. Heard it one too many times, perhaps. It is a bloody good story though.

Why so serious? It's not that big a deal. Boy meets girl, nature takes its course, parents find out, whoops, smack on the wrist, that's that. Yeah, we were a bit young, but it happens every day. Wake up and smell the coffee, as they say.

Oh, I see, you've been talking to Damien. *Now* I see. He has some idea that he was a cause célèbre because of this, that it was a massive tragedy, doesn't he? For goodness' sake. Is he still as pathetic as he used to be? No, that's too harsh. Scratch that from the record. Not pathetic. But there is something a bit sad about Damien, isn't there? A bit... wilted? A bit tears of a clown? Tries too hard. Just that little bit too keen to underline that everything's about him, that he's just extraordinary, just in case you might notice that really – whisper it – there's nothing that remarkable about him at all. I haven't seen him in years but I assume he hasn't changed much. Still making a massive song and dance about nothing. Just for something to do.

You know what's at the root of it all, don't you? Money. Damien always had a gigantic chip on his shoulder about money. That's why he talks in that ridiculous fey sort of way and tries to throw in as many long words as possible. He's trying to compensate for a lack of cash with an abundance of words. If you ask him about class – and really, I wouldn't advise it, because you'll never manage to shut him up – he'll throw out all sorts of pre-prepared speeches about how class is education, and class is vocabulary, and class is really nothing but a question of who bonked whose great great grandfather on the head with an axe and then bonked his woman in the cave or whatnot. But really, if you want to understand Damien, all you really need to know is that he knows class is money, and he's never had any, and it drives him crazy. So he's spent his life looking for cash surrogates. Like words. Or girls. Or notoriety.

Look, since you genuinely appear to be interested – though I can't imagine why – I'll give you an example. When we were all about eight or nine, I got this bike. It was amazing. You know what boys are like with bikes – at that age it's like having the hot blonde girlfriend. It was a red racing bike with a bell and streaks of lightning on the frame. I got it for my birthday. Well, I loved that bike. I used to ride it up and down the road, with Lizzie and Day and whoever else we were hanging out with at the time watching me. I offered them all a go. Taught Lizzie and some others to ride it. But Damien wouldn't touch it. Always said I looked stupid on it. He'd just sit there glowering at me. And one day Lizzie and I were having a particularly good time; I think we were both trying to ride it at the same time. She was standing up behind me with her hands on my shoulders holding on, and we were reeling all over the road, laughing and holding on to each other, and then suddenly something hit me hard in the back. He'd thrown a full can of Coke at me. He stood up and shouted, *You look like dickheads! You look like massive dickheads!* Lizzie started laughing, I don't think she knew what else to do, and Damien burst into tears and ran away.

Well, we felt bad then of course. He was jealous, obviously. Lizzie remembered how funny he was about birthdays and getting new things and stuff, and the two of us realised that he was only pretending to think it was stupid, that he probably wanted a bike more than anything in the world but couldn't admit it because he was poor and couldn't afford one. So I decided that evening that I wouldn't ride it any more, or at least not when he was around. Which I think was pretty big of me, considering I was only eight or nine or whatever it was, and it was the best toy I'd ever had.

But the *point*, the point is this. I left my bike locked up by the side of our house and I didn't ride it from that day onward. My parents were really disappointed. But then, a week or so after this, when we'd made up and it was all forgotten, I checked on my bike, and someone, *someone* had shoved the tyres full of rusty nails.

That's the point about bloody Damien. He can't just suffer you to renounce something. He has to take it from you, even if you've given it up already. Makes him feel like a man, I suppose.

Day

Nick doesn't like me: have you noticed?

Because of the girls, of course. Because of what happened

back then, with Lizzie, and then with Rachel. Nick has an extremely fragile sense of his own masculinity. He always has. He needs to be defined by things, by material possessions – in which he includes women, by the way. And if somebody takes away his *thing*, he basically dissolves and is carried off on the breeze.

We did used to be friends, you know. It must be rather odd, coming at it from your point of view, meeting us all now and trying to figure out what really happened, when it was so long ago and we've all changed so much. But if you can credit it, Nick and I were actually very good friends, until it all happened. It will, I hope, become clear why I fell out with him – I had ample reasons for doing so. He and Lizzie between them, after all, tried to get me put behind bars. Which is not exactly what you expect of your *friends*.

I wonder what I liked about him now, before it all happened. That is something, I'm afraid, that hasn't survived very well in my mind. Maybe he can tell you. Maybe the others can.

We keep digressing, don't we? I hope I'm not the only one who does this. Have the others been rambling all over the place too? It's hard, you see, to tell the story straight because there's so much background. There's also so much *foreground*. And all of it different, I'll warrant, depending on who you're talking to. Everyone knows there's no such thing as truth nowadays. What's that line? It's in that exquisite Robbie Williams and Gary Barlow duet, where they made up and they're gay cowboys. *There's three versions of this story, mine and yours and then the truth.* They probably weren't the first to say it, but they did say it so beautifully. Well, anyway, we're well beyond that now. You'll be lucky if you come away from this with less than twenty or thirty versions of the story, and best of luck piecing the truth together from *that*.

Incidentally, speaking of Gary and Robbie, you could do worse than to consider Nick and I broadly along the lines of those two great frenemies of the Nineties and Noughties. The parallels are rather striking, actually. I, needless to say, am a Robbie. Exploding across the celebrity stratosphere in a dazzling shower of infamy, eloquence, addiction, helplessness, bravado, vulnerability. Irritating quite a number of people along the way, I grant you, but never ignorable, never forgettable! Nick, of course, is a Gary. Solid, plodding, safe pair of hands, unsexy as threadbare socks kept on during copulation, but *underestimate him at your peril*. For, while Robbie was snorting coke off backing dancers' perineums and setting the charts alight, Gary was squatting in his cave plotting his revenge; writing anodyne ditties for cardboard cut-out boy bands, counting his pennies, slowly amassing a reputation in the music business, building up a pap pop empire brick by stealthy brick. When Robbie finally burned out, Gary emerged at the forefront of a newly formed Take That, porky finger in every pie in the music business, head of his own record label. Now look at him, being a judge on *The X Factor*, all gimlet eye and chiseled chin. Ruling the world. It wasn't long before poor, reduced, drug-addled Robbie was begging for a slice of the nostalgia pie.

I would never have re-joined the band. Shame on you, Robbie. You caved. You sold out.

God, I've done it again. Okay, look, let's talk dates and places. I can remember the dates. The first week of August, 1997. Particularly the Saturday to the Monday. There. I've done my bit. Rachel can fill you in on the places.

Rachel
You want to know about Chesterton Close? Well, there's not much to tell. Day always thought it was a fascinating area, some kind of melting pot of cultures and classes, but I'm not sure it was anything special. Just a pretty standard suburban street. Mostly semi-detached houses, boxy brick red affairs with nondescript front gardens and slightly bigger but

also unremarkable back gardens. Trees were planted on the pavements, and had obviously been badly planned because the roots had started to split the tarmac and make it all bumpy. Quite a lot of litter.

Oh, I don't know. I'm bad with atmosphere. I remember people.

It was a cul-de-sac, though, I do remember that much. And one end of it, the open end of it that led onto the main road, was much nicer than the closed end, because that was where the council estate started, and the final block of the council flats was where Day lived. My house was sort of halfway down the road. Lizzie's house a little bit further, but they were close by, you could see her front door from mine. And then, the nice end was where Nick lived. He had a wall, and stone lions on the gateposts, shoddy crumbly things that looked like they were slightly disgusted rather than roaring, but they were pretty impressive to kids.

Day once told me that when Nick came round to his house for the first time, when they were really little, long before I knew them, he turned to Day when they walked into the main communal bit of the flats and said, *Oh. Don't you have lions on your gateposts?* I'm not sure if I believe that, though. Do you? Seems pretty insensitive, even for a very young kid.

We didn't go round to Day's much. At all. He always came to ours. But, as we found out later, there were reasons for that.

So, I don't know, what else do you need to know? There was a corner shop, well we called it that but actually it was well around the corner, down the main road. That was pretty important to us as kids but again, looking back it was just your standard newsagents. Newspapers, mags, sweets and chocolate, cigarettes, a Walls ice cream fridge with one of those slidey tops. We used to buy ice pops a lot, that summer, before it all happened. The red ones were the best.

The parish church was bang smack opposite my house.

Look, it's not about the geography of it. This could have taken place on any street in the country. It's about the *people* involved, the psychology of it. Specifically, it's about the bizarre attitude that Catholics have towards sex. That's why the fallout happened, really. Day and Lizzie, it was just crossed wires. Nick didn't mean to make things worse either, he was scared and just said what he thought he remembered. It was the grown-ups that made things worse, them and the bloody priest. Have you met Father Patrick yet? Interfering old... busybody, isn't he? Watch out for him, he'll be keeping an eye on you. He keeps an eye on everyone. He loves it.

There – did you see what I just did there? I'm still calling him *Father*, and I called him a *busybody*, which is a word you don't find outside Enid Blyton books these days, because that's the worst I could bring myself to say. When what I really meant to say is that Patrick Creevey is an interfering old prick. But being brought up Catholic does this to you. It works on your language, it restrains you, it forces you to be respectful of things you don't respect. You can be as rational a person as you like in normal everyday things, and yet when it comes to calling a priest a prick, or speaking loudly in a church, or something like that, you can't help but cringe and regress. So people say, *Ah there's no harm in people being religious if it makes them happy,* but people don't know what being religious does to them. That's the problem.

It's the same with sex as it is with language. Being brought up Catholic fucks you up, sexually speaking, for the rest of your life. Oh, it's not like we *abstain*. Kids will be kids. I think it's impossible to not have sex in the world we live in today, unless you're so unattractive you can't find anyone who'll have you, and then there's always prostitution. But the Catholic thing doesn't go away, is the point. They sort of coexist, the sex thing and the Catholic thing, pulling you in different directions, *fucking you up*. So we're probably more unhappy in the long run than we'd have been if we'd just abstained in the first place.

Oh, I'm not explaining this very well. Okay, me, for example. I like to think I've got away from this pretty well in general, compared to friends from a similar background. I've had a reasonable but not an outrageous number of sexual partners. I'm definitely not a prude. I'm careful with contraception. But sometimes I'll get this guilt and shame, over nothing at all. Like, the couple of times I had a one-night stand. Nothing wrong with that as long as you use protection, but I felt so dirty the next day. I scrubbed myself until it hurt. I kept thinking of how upset Dad would be if he knew – I mean, what's *that* about? I try to avoid them now. One-night stands, I mean. If I stick to sex in a relationship, in *my* relationship, then I can ignore it, generally speaking.

But this is nothing compared to friends' stories. You know, friends with the same kind of upbringing. I've got one friend who always cries after sex, she told me. Not much, and she usually tries to go to the bathroom to keep it discreet, try not to freak her boyfriend out. But she says she always feels like a whore, because she enjoyed it. And then she's seized by a massive panic that she'll never get married, because nobody would marry a whore who puts out. I've got another friend who's never had an orgasm in her life. She's just accepted it, she thinks women aren't meant to, that they're just there to be impregnated. This same friend once told me that she can't wait till she gets married and gets pregnant, because then she'll *never need to have sex again*. Is this *normal*? Is this *okay*?

Try this on for size:

> Keep away from fornication. All the other sins are committed outside the body; but to fornicate is to sin against your own body. Your body, you know, is the temple of the Holy Spirit, who is in you since you receive him from God. You are not your own property; you have been bought and paid for. That is why you should use your body for the glory of God.

St. Paul to the Corinthians, that is. *Bought and paid for.*

Fuck it, ask *Lizzie* what she thinks about sex. Well, she might not tell you. She's a bit shy about it these days, which is funny – I don't mean funny, I mean sad – considering how she used to be. Growing up with a mum like hers, though, she had no chance of not being fucked up.

Have you met Lizzie's mum yet? Lizzie's mum – and I do not use this word lightly – is a *cunt*.

Nick

So, we were fourteen. It was the summer, and school had finished. And it had been coming for a while, I suppose. Day had been sniffing around Lizzie for God knows how long, and I think they'd had some sort of wanky-pokey in the cinema or something. And when she wasn't around, he'd been prancing about making lewd jokes about getting his end away. I wasn't jealous. I mean, no offence to Lizzie, but she wasn't really... I wasn't that bothered about her. I suppose when I was younger I had a bit of a crush on her, probably because she was the only girl I really knew because our parents were friendly, and you know what you're like at that age. But by that point, by that summer, I was looking elsewhere. I was looking for something more interesting. Someone with a bit more to them. More of a challenge.

I found Rachel.

I still speak to her, you know, every now and then, but it's a bit awkward. We've not got much to say. She always suggests meeting up, but I'm pretty busy these days and it's hard to find the time. I think she wants to talk about it all, actually. The whole business of what happened that summer. I don't know why she can't move on from all this. I think Rachel's problem is she doesn't like throwing people away. Whereas, the way I see it, you have to throw people out as you move through life. To make room for all the new people. Like cleaning out the garage or something. You're never going to have enough space for everything. You've got to choose.

But I wouldn't totally get rid of Rachel, even though we've got practically nothing in common any more. You've always got a soft spot for your first. I know she's got one for me.

Plus, she's attractive. Isn't she?

What would you say is attractive about Rachel? I'm genuinely interested. I think it's a very hard question to answer. She's not stereotypically gorgeous. She's certainly not *hot*, you know. Like my wife, Chrissy, she's a stunning woman. Ha. Yes. No, Rachel's not like that at all. You might not give her a second glance until you talk to her. But, there is something about her.

So you can understand why I sometimes forget to mention to Chrissy that I spoke to Rachel, when we do catch up. Oh, I'm straight as an arrow, don't get me wrong. But Chrissy gets jealous. Hell hath no fury and all that. But I don't mind, you know? That's part of being married. Actually, I think that's one of the nicest things about being married.

Lizzie

Just one thing. Just one thing I want to set the record straight on. The bike. Cos if you get that, you'll get it all.

I stuck the nails in Nick's bike tyres. I got them from my dad's garage, and I went round there when everyone was at church and did it. It seems a stupid thing to do now, especially since all Nick would have needed to do was get a new pair of tyres. Stupid and pointless. But it seemed important at the time, back when I thought that if you liked someone you should act like you liked them.

If you tell him that, I'll kill you.

Paul

Hello there. Look, I'll get straight to the point. I'm only going to say this to you once. And I'm only saying it at all because

I know for a fact you've been talking to my ex-wife. If you're going round talking to people about what happened back then, you should at least have both sides of the story.

It wasn't Lizzie's fault.

For God's sake. I can't believe I even have to say that.

It was the last straw for me. With Kathleen, I mean. With the whole thing. There had been problems for years... but I was weak, I suppose, and I didn't want trouble, and I wanted to make it work. Marriage was always a big thing for me. A serious thing, not just a word, not something to be treated lightly. So I shut my eyes to things. To so many things. But this was the last straw.

I remember exactly how it happened, the very moment. We were sitting around the kitchen table, the three of us. It was raining outside and we had the lights on in the kitchen. The potatoes were boiling. Lizzie was crying, crying her eyes out, and Kathleen just sat there and *looked* at her. Judging her. She wouldn't give her a cuddle, she wouldn't tell her it was okay. And then she turned to me and shook her head and sort of rolled her eyes as if to say at the same time, *You don't believe her do you?* and *I saw it coming.* For me, it was like – you'll have to forgive me, I'm not good at putting these things – it was like something fell away from my eyes at that moment. I couldn't stay there a moment longer. I took Lizzie in my arms and cuddled her, and then I took her hand and got her coat. It was raining that day, I think I told you, even though it was summer. It was a bad summer. And I took her down to the police station in the car. I remember, I remember watching the rain beat against the windscreen and the wipers washing it away, and I wiped Kathleen out of my mind just like that, and she was gone. I could shut my eyes to some things. But not to my daughter curled up on the back seat of the car crying her eyes out, because she got raped and her own mother didn't believe her.

Kathleen

Then why didn't she tell us before they found the keys, before we got the call? Answer me that, why don't you?

Sometimes the worst thing you can do as a parent is to shut your eyes to what your children are. That's something Paul has never been able to understand.

Let me tell you something. Children always have a favourite parent, in much the way that parents always have a favourite child. You're not allowed to say that, of course, but it doesn't stop it being true. Well, I always knew that Paul was her favourite. Ironic, under the circumstances, isn't it? You could tell from the beginning, when she was a baby. She first smiled at him. Not me. She took her first step for him. Not me. She would draw him pictures and pick my flowers and give them to him, and all that sort of thing. She was sly about it. About getting him on her side, so she could do no wrong in his eyes. And then making me look bad.

She once said to me, when she was five or six, *Mam, am I adopted?*

No, I said. I said it calmly. *What a silly idea. Who's been putting that into your head?*

Are you sure I'm yours though? she said. *Not Daddy's and some other lady's?*

How would you feel, if your daughter turned round and said that to you?

She was sitting at the kitchen table, eating a yoghurt, with the sunlight making her hair gleam. Looking ever so sweet and adorable, with this horrible stuff coming out of her mouth. I wanted to shake her. To tell her the truth about where she came from and see her prattle about being adopted then. Of course, I didn't, I just told her not to be stupid and gave her some colouring to do.

You'll think I'm making it up, I suppose. Or exaggerating. That I was just neurotic. That's what Paul once worked his way up to telling me, once, when I'd got furious with her because I was the one putting in the bloody hours, slaving away to feed her and dress her and play with her and educate her, and she'd be a little bloody nightmare all day. She has violence in her. You'd never know to look at her, so quiet as she sits there for company. For anyone but me. But trust me, it's there. When she was nine or ten even, that sort of age, she'd lie on the floor and just scream, for hours on end, if I wouldn't give her whatever it was she wanted. And then he'd come in at the end of the day and it'd be all smiles and cuddles and *Daddy this* and *Daddy that*.

So he was soft on her as a consequence. I had to take care of all the discipline. And then he'd undo all the good that I did. By telling me not to be hard on her whenever she blubbered. By undermining me. By indulging her bad habits.

Day

Good God, they're all as bad as me, aren't they? You may have an idea by now of exactly what you've taken on. I pity you, poor soul. Let me lighten your load. Pour yourself a stiff drink – this is what happened.

It was the four of us, and it was the summer holidays. We had spent the earlier part of it doing what kids do. Being bored. Going to the cinema in town to see the vapid summer blockbusters, and menacing younger kids on the swings in the park, and plotting ways to get drunk. Best of all, though, we liked hanging around on the street. Write that down and take it home, by the way. It's my adolescent self's free gift to you. Grown-ups always think that their offspring hang around on the street because they don't have anything else to do. That couldn't be further from the truth. There was *plenty* to do in our neighbourhood. There was the parish youth club, for example. There were sports teams and a swimming pool ten minutes away at the council leisure centre. There was the television and there were computer games and books – well, there were books in Nick and Rachel's houses anyway. My point is, what else there is to do has nothing whatsoever to do with why kids hang around on street corners. They do it because they've figured out that it's intimidating, and they like it. When grown-ups walk by, grown-ups by themselves, they're not exactly scared but they shut down a little, they tense, they brace themselves in case you're trouble, in case you're going to hassle them. Nick and I were quite big for our age. It's a powerful feeling. There's nothing like a taste of power when you're fourteen.

And sex had recently taken over my head. Nick and I had been talking about it a lot, you know, as you do, when you've started buying *FHM* and *Loaded*, and making the link between the zeppelin-breasted deities of the top shelf and the real girls that you know, and suddenly you realise that the two worlds could collide, and you could *actually have sex* and it takes over your life.

Now, I had been kissing Lizzie that summer, in the cinema and behind the shed in her back garden, and anywhere else I could manage it. I can't remember when I first started liking her, and wanting to kiss her, and doing stuff for her like opening her ice pops. Probably years before. But early that summer, she let me kiss her, and we kissed whenever we could.

Would you like the gory details? One evening, behind her shed, she let me put my hand on her little breast, and then she let me pull up the fabric of her top – cheap, deliciously cheap, a peach-coloured halter top from New Look, I remember it well – and slip my hand underneath it to feel her heated and tightening flesh. The air was warm and still like that of a foreign country, and the birds were doing that summer cooing cry in the trees at the front of the house. Her mouth was near my ear and she was making no sound, just breathing slowly and regularly as if she was taking a lie detector test. My ear thrilled to every measured breath, sending tingles down my neck, through my chest. I thought, *I can do it. I can do it.* I moved my hand and dug my fingers down her shorts, they were tight so it was hard to push my whole hand in, and then I put my index and middle fingers into the bits of her I'd been dreaming about, that disgusting fascinating weird female place. She was so hot there, not as wet as I expected though, just hot, and she tensed and tightened but didn't make a sound. Just that ready, regular breathing. She could have been anywhere. I didn't know what to do so I just poked my fingers around for a bit. Then I said, *I want to fuck you*, and she said something I couldn't hear, and I said, *What*, and she said, *Yeah*.

I went and told Nick straight afterwards, of course. Went round to his house to tell him. I'm afraid he was distraught. Because, you know, Nick fancied Lizzie as well at that point. Of course he did. Lizzie was made for fourteen-year-old boys to fancy. She looked like a little Disney princess and didn't talk very much, and that's a combination to make the adolescent male heart flutter and organ swell if there ever was one. I don't mean to brag, but the two of us had seemingly spent forever vying to impress her, and then I got ahead when I fingered her behind the shed and Nick was consumed with jealousy. He hadn't even kissed a girl until then. And he's very competitive, you know. He needs validation. So, the next day, he brought Rachel to hang around with us after the mass.

You can tell a lot about Nick from one little fact, you know, which is this. His parents paid him for his grades at school. I don't just mean that if he got full marks on a spelling test, they'd give him something or other. I mean, his dad worked out a proper system. A sliding scale. If he got 20 out of 20, they gave him a pound. 19 out of 20 was worth 80p. 18 out of 20 was worth 60p. And so on.

And if he got below a 15, he had to pay *them*.

I always imagined them sitting there in Nick's dad's study, every Saturday morning, with young Nicholas, cowlick wetted down and shining face, tremblingly presenting a pile of pristine exercise books for Pater's approval. Pater sorts through them gravely, adding to his tally in a leather-bound notebook as he goes, eventually totting up the sums and pronouncing the grand total boomingly, like unto the Metatron pronouncing Judgement Day. Little Nicky basks in fatherly approval or writhes in agony 'neath the scorching glare of disappointment, generally depending on whether I had seen fit to help him with his homework that week or not. Usually, Pater produces a note, or a few coins, with a sombre injunction not to spend it all at once, and away Little Nicky capers to hoard the cash in his piggy bank. He actually had a piggy bank, by the way. A money box shaped like a pig.

I shouldn't tease. Nick was our banker. It was only thanks to his parents' slightly bizarre mode of parental 'support' that we had the money to carry out the plan.

Anyway, sorry. You wanted to know about Lizzie and instead I've obtruded the ungainly form of Nick onto your retina. An ungracious substitution on my part; my apologies. So, Lizzie and I were getting hot and heavy and Nick was jealous, and so I suppose he brought Rachel in to catch up, and then we started thinking along the same lines. We decided it was about time we had sex. It was the beginning of August.

Lizzie

I was different, back then, you know. I had Nick and Day, they were, like, my boys. We did everything together.

I can't even remember how it all began. When we were little. I think Day and Nick went to primary school together, and then my parents were friends with Nick's parents, so we all played together and stuff. I remember playing in the sandpit in the summer, and in the winter the three of us having tea round at mine or Nick's. Fish fingers and chips, or party tea if we were extra lucky. Watching videos. Birthday parties. Nick's birthday parties were the best. He had a ball pool once.

But it changed that summer. When Rachel came along,

but actually even before that. It felt like the boys were starting to fall out more, get jealous of each other. I don't want to be boastful or anything, but I knew it was to do with me. I had started to realise, around that time, that – this makes me sound dead full of myself, but I don't mean it like that – well, that blokes fancied me. I don't mean just boys, Day and Nick or the boys at school or whatever, either. I mean, like, men. Proper men. I'd have men come and talk to me on the bus and in the shops and that. Even when I was in my school uniform. Ask me about myself. Ask for my phone number. Try to give me theirs. Ask me to meet them on Friday night, ask to walk me home. I never did it, 'cause I didn't know them and all that, and anyway my mum would've gone mad. But you know, it was nice. It's nice to get attention when you're young. Makes you feel like you're worth something.

And Day and Nick both liked me, I could tell. Maybe they always had. Or maybe it was just that summer that they started liking me. But something had changed. They started trying to impress me. Nick would try and buy me things. Like, a teddy bear or a CD or something. Day, it was harder to pin down. I guess it was like, he was so disdainful of most of the world that it felt amazing that he was soft to me. I felt special. I didn't do much about either of them at first. They would both try and brush against me walking along, or touch my leg in the cinema or whatever.

I'd always loved Day though. Like, the stuff with the bike. So, I was always going to pick him.

Then Rachel came along.

I would never have seen it coming, you know. I mean, I was even surprised that Nick picked her when me and Day started being properly together. She had lived on our street for ages, but none of us had really noticed her, I don't think. The boys had never mentioned her anyway. She was… urgh, you're going to think I'm really mean when I say this, but… she was kind of *fat*.

Nick

I don't really remember exactly how Rachel got involved, if I'm honest with you. Like I said, I had clocked her for a while, thought she was nice looking and all that. I think we just got talking after mass one day, if I remember right. Then she started hanging out with us. I could tell she liked me, so I thought why not? And things went from there.

And yeah. It was… nice. It felt like everything had fallen into place. Day and Lizzie. Me and Rachel.

Rachel

Let's get something straight about what teenage girls find attractive, okay? It's not what adults think. There's always that boy in the class, isn't there, the good-looking sporty one with blond hair in curtains, and the teachers assume that he's the one who would be a hit with the little ladies. Well, generally, he's not. It's the funny boy who turns them on. Nothing like the alchemy of laughter. When it occurs to you, as a teenage girl, that there's such a bank of entertainment all stored up in one person, you fall straight in love with him. Laughter's like magic. It's not about looks at all. That's what I think, anyway.

So, Nick is actually… I don't know, I guess you'd say good-looking, but that's not what I'm trying to put across. He was sort of golden back then. You know those yellow chickens in the supermarket that cost twice as much as the pale, bloody ones? It says they're corn-fed. Well, he had that corn-fed look too. Good genes. Brought up on balanced meals and frequent outdoor exercise, with snacks of fruit and mineral water. And nice clothes. His parents couldn't do enough for him, and they had money, and the money and the love sort of shone out of his pores. I've heard he's a bit jowly these days (don't tell him I said that), but back then he was, well, he was what he was. Which I suppose I should call good-looking, seeing as I can't seem to put it effectively in any other way.

41

Whereas Day looked ridiculous. He always has done. But that's not what it's about, with him.

In church, I used to look at the three of them sitting on the radiator. They always sat the same way. One of the boys on either side, with Lizzie in the middle. Nick was impassive, solemn, always staring straight ahead. Looking at whatever he was supposed to be looking at. Day was like some kind of ridiculous ugly gremlin, with his gap-toothed grin and stupid hair sticking up everywhere and his clothes that were too big or too small, looking around, looking everywhere, always, for a new audience.

Lizzie was… beautiful. Scary. Sitting in the middle, like some sort of superstar flanked by her bodyguards, not looking at anything in particular at all.

You know who's clever? Kate Moss is clever. I've always thought this. She's a beautiful woman, sure, but not that beautiful. Not *the world's* most beautiful woman. There are so many others, coming and going like fashion, who actually, aesthetically, are more beautiful than Kate Moss. But you know how she manages to keep everyone fascinated, to keep everyone worshipping her? Keeping her mouth shut. She's managed to create a cult around herself through keeping her mouth shut. We're all just desperate to know about her, and she won't give us what we're looking for. Still, now she's forty or whatever, she hardly says a word. We have to rummage around in 'anonymous pals' and 'a source close to Kate' for our wild speculations, and she just smiles and never says a word. So we love her.

You can probably tell what I'm getting at. That's how I saw Lizzie. I got to know her better afterwards, but I never quite knew her. I still don't.

Anyway. Nick came up to me one day after mass. I was hanging around in the pews at the back, waiting for Dad to finish his schmoozing with all the powerful old men who played golf, and Nick came up and said, awkwardly, *Alright*. I did that classic thing of looking over my shoulder to see who he was speaking to, because naturally he couldn't have been talking to me, but there was nobody there. I turned back around and suddenly I realised I had to say something back to him, so I said, *Alright, yeah.* Then we stood there for a bit and he said, *You're Rachel, right?* And I said, *Yeah,* and he said, *I'm Nick* and I said, *I know.* It was not a dazzling dialogue by any stretch of the imagination. I was amazed, awestruck. My heart was going like anything. Eventually he said I could come and hang out with them that evening, if I wanted to, and I said, *Okay, what time?* and he just shrugged as if time had never mattered to him. And then Dad came out and I said, *Bye,* in a hurry, and went to join him.

And on the way home I said to Dad, *Can I go and hang out with some friends after dinner?* He said, *Which friends?* Quite understandable. I didn't have any friends in the neighbourhood. I had a few friends at school, fat scholarly girls like me. But none of them lived in Sale. So Dad said, *Who?* And I said, *Oh, Lizzie O'Leary. She asked me.* And Dad said, *Oh, yes, Paul's daughter. Okay.*

I said Lizzie had asked me, not Nick. Even though I hadn't even spoken to her yet. See, that, that's the kind of thing I'm talking about. That's what being a Catholic does to you.

So I went and hung out with them. We sat on the wall outside Nick's house and ate our ice pops, and talked about people at school, and films we'd seen and wanted to see, and all that kind of stuff. I could tell that I was there for Nick. Little attentions that he paid me. I couldn't believe it at first. After we'd finished that evening, when dusk was falling and Lizzie's mum started calling for her from the front door, I went home and walked upstairs and into my room, and shut the door. Then I took off all my clothes and looked in the mirror at my own unlovely reflection, and marveled at what he could possibly find in it to like. I thought it must be a mistake on my part. I went to bed clenching my fists into the dark and telling myself not to be stupid, not to get my hopes up. Not to be so full of myself.

But it was unmistakable. Nick liked me. He had sat next to me and his leg had touched mine and he had asked me stuff. And then, a few days later, in the cinema, he kissed me.

And I liked him, because he liked me. It's a great unromantic truth, this, that this is just how attraction works sometimes. People make a lot of the opposite kind of attraction don't they, the Women Love Bastards school of thought, the venerable Treat 'Em Mean, Keep 'Em Keen tradition. But I don't know if I buy it… there's at least as much to be said for the converse. Especially when you're young. When you don't think people give a crap about you, you don't really feel that much about them – it's self-defence really, like, *Screw you then, I don't like you either*. But if you find out they do like you… you think softly about them and the thought of their pining lights up your day, and you start to find things about them interesting that you never did before. 'Flattered', I think, has always been an utterly inadequate word for that sweet, sexy explosion of pleasure in your head. A flat, cardboard sort of word for the feeling that brings an inanimate world to life. And you never feel it more sharply than when you're fourteen years old and just growing out of puppy fat.

Maybe it's just me. Or maybe it's everyone, but most people don't want to admit it. Because it doesn't give the most flattering picture of ourselves, if we confess that we find somebody more attractive if they'll have us. It implies, doesn't it, that we want to be needed. That we need to be wanted. That the stuff we're made up of is only as good as its market price.

Of course, it was Day I was in love with. I suppose that's obvious. But I *liked* Nick. And more importantly, he liked me. I saw no incompatibility between the way I felt about the two of them.

And I wasn't jealous of Lizzie, believe it or not. Falling in love with somebody who's already into someone else is actually very underrated. You start from the point that they will never be yours, and then every word, every look, every moment of connection is a bonus from that baseline. So I kissed Nick and thought of Day. I went to see Day, and sat next to Nick. And when Day suggested the plan, I went along with it happily because it came from his head and if he'd suggested I throw myself under a bus, I'd have said, *What number?* The fact that the plan involved losing my virginity to Nick, not Day, was neither here nor there.

Day

Shall I tell you something? Something I've never told anyone? Except Rachel, of course.

I didn't have to go to mass like the others. But I pretended that I did.

There were several services every Sunday in our parish, but the evening service – at 5.30, I think it was – was the most popular. Largely because this tradition had sprung up at some point of sitting at the back. You know, everyone went there in their families and the parents would go and sit at the front of the church in the pews, and all the teenagers would sit at the back and gossip and moan quietly about having to be there, and snigger at the grown-ups singing. It was sort of an accepted deal between the adult community and the teenage community. Enforced presence. Tolerated sociability.

Well, I pretended my mum made me go, like all the others. I moaned about what a massive drag it was and rolled my eyes and even sometimes pretended she was sitting somewhere up at the front with my brother. But she didn't, and she wasn't. My mum never had a shadow of a clue where I was, and wouldn't have given a flying fuck if she'd known. No, I went to mass because I *liked* it.

I don't really know why I liked it. Rachel was horrified the first time I told her that – she spent most of her life trying to get out of going, I think, and it would have been bliss for her to be let off the hook. Sometimes I told her I liked watching people, everyone offered up for inspection like that. Sometimes I told her that I liked the atmosphere, the incense and all the meditation-friendly rumbling and chanting and the dulcet tones of our Father Patrick. Like a spa soundtrack or something. And once I tried to explain to her how if somebody tries to make you do something then you don't want to do it of course; but how if nobody gives a flying fuck whether you do it or not, then you find to your great surprise that you actually want to do it more than anything. That was the real reason, but I'm not sure she got it. She sets a great deal of store by liberty. Perhaps not enough, to my way of thinking, by confinement.

Rachel and the mass. The mass and Rachel. My eternal image of *her*, when I think back to the time when it all went wrong, is of her standing up there doing the Reading. It gave me a great opportunity, every third Sunday or so, to watch her. I had done so for years. Not for her looks; I had the best-looking girl I knew sitting beside me coltishly rubbing her calf against mine, and anyway, with Rachel it wasn't really about the looks. No, what I liked about Rachel was her anger. The way that I could tell, through the dissembling veil of her perfect diction and calm gaze – she looked up at the end of every sentence – that she was angry at the world. At our world. The congregation, the street outside the church, the town outside the street – she hated it all. She went a marvellous colour up there. A beautiful shade of rage.

I don't remember quite when I first started noticing this. I don't really remember when I first saw her, spoke to her, when we declared ourselves. The origins of our relationship are murky in my mind, one sighting or conversation blurring into another and becoming a rainbowed rush of how things were. All you need to know is that the colour of her cheeks, Sunday after

Sunday after Sunday, is one more point from which I trace the arc of our enterprise, and the source of my tragedy.

Michel

My mother, God rest her soul, used to have lots of little catchphrases. One of them was, *Si à vingt ans tu n'es pas de gauche c'est que tu n'as pas de coeur; si tu l'est toujours à quarante ans, c'est que tu n'as pas de tête!* Or, in English, it translates like this: *If you're not a socialist when you're twenty, you have no heart. If you're still a socialist when you're forty, you have no head!* It sounds better in the French, though, in my opinion.

My mother was a clever woman, even though she spent all of her life as a housewife. One is not supposed to say that sort of thing, right? But I think you know what I mean. If things had been different in her time, I think she could have done something great. She might have been a philosopher, or something like that. Made the thoughts in her head into something permanent. As it was, she spent her life making soups and stews and beds and temporary peace. They are all nice things, but they pass away. The only place where her thoughts have lived on is in my head. They live there still, even now that I am nearly sixty. I close my eyes and I can see her sitting in her chair with her book in the evenings, when she got a rare moment of peace, and looking up at me suddenly, sharply, and saying this or that or the other. She understood the world. That is to say, she had an understanding of the world that satisfied her. In my opinion, that makes her a clever woman.

But the point I want to make is that I don't think she had that one entirely right. The catchphrase, I mean. *At twenty years old, you have no heart,* and so on. At least, I don't think that she had it right when it came to her son. I don't understand why, but I have come to think that I became steadily less and less conservative as I grew older. Now, why do you suppose that is?

Conservative with a small c, I mean. I'm not talking about

politics. Well, I am, but not in the sense of different parties. Just in the way that involves how you live your life.

I would say that I was probably most conservative when Rachel was born. That is now, what do you call it, a truism, isn't it? The idea that having children makes you conservative. I suppose because you want to make the world safe for them, so you get very keen on law and order. And you want to build up money to provide things for them, so you start to resent being taxed, because it feels like your money is being taken from your child to give it to other people's children instead. I have felt this, this kind of noble selfishness. I know what it's like.

The real question in my mind is, why didn't it last? Because I experienced this short burst of that kind of emotion, which lasted maybe two or three years, and then it started to drain away. As Rachel grew older, all my principles started to ring hollow in my ears. Being a father made me feel less authoritative, not more. My certainties vanished.

They called me Michael, by the way, but my real name is Michel. I'm French, you see. You might have noticed. When I say 'they', by the way, I mean everybody in the neighbourhood did, when we lived in England, at the time. Now I'm back in France, I am Michel again. Rachel still calls me Michael though. It is a deliberate decision with her. Everything she does is deliberate.

We get on well. It is hard not to get along with Rachel, if you ask me, although I know I am biased. She is so determined to understand everybody. Even when they don't deserve it. Sometimes I want to tell her, *Be crueler. Be more discriminating.* I worry, sometimes, that her determination to understand everybody will hurt her in some way. It can be a valuable quality to see things in black and white – in two simple dimensions, you might say. If you try to see every point of view, to give it equal validity, you can find yourself living in an impossible world. Like one of those Picasso paintings with a million different dimensions, where everything is split up. It feels like my life has become more like that, as I've got older. More interesting, but more painful. Rachel has always been like that. Maybe she taught me to be like that, in some way I haven't yet quite understood.

My wife died of breast cancer when Rachel was eight years old. It's been hard sometimes, sure. There are still so many things that are reserved for women to talk about. How do you explain to her about periods when you've never had one? How do you tell her about boys, and what they want, and how they will behave unless you're careful? I tried my best, after Roberta was gone. When Rachel was young, we used to sit in the living room in the evenings, watching television, me with a glass of wine, and her with a glass of juice. And when the adverts came on I would try to tell her things. Try to parcel up the little bits of wisdom I had accumulated over my life and give them to her all wrapped and ready to go. Like that thing I just said about paintings. She used to look at me as if I was mad.

As she got older, I started to give her a proper drink of her own. She liked that. First of all I'd let her dip her finger in my glass of wine and suck it. Then she was allowed a sip. When she was ten or so, I would let her have a little, what do you call it, like a shot glass full of a sweet cherry liqueur that I kept in the cabinet. Then when she became a teenager, she was allowed her own small glass of wine. When I gave her drinks, I felt like I was giving her wisdom, helping her to be grown-up. Maybe that made it easier to avoid really talking to her, talking to her in the way that she needed.

It was especially difficult to give her any advice about love. I didn't know how to counsel her. I had feelings of course, I remember embarrassing incidents when I was growing up, but… nothing like what happened with Rachel, the thing you want to know about. I sometimes think the past was more innocent. But not necessarily in a good way.

I should have been angry, I suppose, when it happened. But I felt helpless instead. I didn't feel like I had any right to comment. I think maybe that was the end of my conservatism.

They were all so angry with me. Paul, the father of Lizzie. *You don't seem to care at all,* he kept saying, and I was sorry for him, because it was a different thing with his daughter. But he had reported it to the police, and that was that, so what did he expect me to do? I was not keen to get any more wrapped up in that family than I already was. I was already... well, I'm sure you have heard about this. No need for me to go over old ground. Let sleeping dogs lie, as they say.

Rachel

So, that summer, I became Nick's girlfriend. Usually we just hung out with the others, but we did do some things by ourselves. Quite soon after we met, he asked me if I wanted to come round to his house. To meet his parents, I realised, the moment that I pressed the doorbell and the door immediately opened and all three of them were standing there in the hall.

After the dinner they propped us up in front of the massive telly with some videos and popcorn and left us to it. His mum made a big fuss about how they'd be upstairs, so call them if we wanted them but otherwise we wouldn't see them. So I expected he'd leap on me as soon as they closed the door. But, no, we just watched this film all the way through, sitting there politely next to each other on the sofa. Then I went home.

It did get a bit easier. There were more nights like that. When we'd kiss and stuff, and one time he put his hand up my top. But that was it.

Day

We were sitting on the kerb eating ice pops. It should have been a sultry summer evening, I suppose, for the ideal atmosphere, but in fact it was just after lunchtime. Early afternoon. The neighbourhood was silent, except for the buzz of the radio coming from somewhere far away, and a dog making a noise in a garden nearby, panting. We definitely had ice pops then. Someone had just said something, and then there was one of those moments of silence where everyone happened to be sucking their ice pops at once. I was looking at Lizzie's legs, kicked out from the kerb, crossed at the ankles. The skin on her legs was always very opaque, especially when sunburned. It looked like pink-brown wax. Smooth and unreal. The sun came out from behind a cloud and what had been a lukewarm sort of afternoon suddenly became dazzlingly hot. The smell of the tarmac. The long call of a bird. The cheerful crackling wisps of radio, and the dog panting, whimpering, then it stopped. And then we heard the sex.

Someone was having sex, in the afternoon, in a house with an open window on the Close. It was the woman's voice mainly. A sound, rhythmic, overpowered, caught somewhere between a breath and a soft shriek. It came like a heartbeat.

I looked at the others. They were listening too. Lizzie smiled a slow smile, and I caught a glimpse of her ice-bruised tongue as her lips parted.

I said, *I think it's about time we did it.*

And that was how it started.

Lizzie

I said it to him behind the shed, I was like, *Let's do it this summer.*

Rachel

I said, *You know what'd really fuck them off?* I said it to him in church one day, for a joke. I think he remembered it. I'd been thinking it for ages.

One reason I wanted to do it was the Reading, and one was to please Day. And I soon got another reason. The best and worst reason.

Nick

Can't even remember how we came up with the idea, to be honest. We'd probably seen a film or something. Was *American Pie* out that summer? That was probably it.

Look, it was silly. Good lord, when I see fourteen-year-olds these days... they're children. Babies. They're not ready. *We* weren't ready. But you are silly, aren't you, when you're that age? You've got to make mistakes in order to learn about life. Take me, for example. I only learned about real love, what a real relationship is like, through having had all this other stuff happen to me. I'm happy now.

Day

You remember, I presume, that I told you Nick was our banker. All those Saturday mornings submitting his piles of leaden comprehensions and laborious integers to his parents finally amounted to *something worth having* when I had my idea. Because we were, of course, going to need money in order to do it right.

It's the sad thing about life in general, isn't it? The thing about money is, it's got all sorts of charms up its sleeve that you might not initially expect. As I've grown older, I've come to understand this, but it's been a rather unpleasant learning curve. Money can, for example, buy you learning, in the shape of that great bleeping, flashing it's-my-birthday badge, a DEGREE. And if learning is knowledge, and knowledge is power, it follows – does it not? – that money can buy you those things too. It can buy you time. It can buy you distance. It can buy you silence. I have learned all of these things, mostly the hard way, since I was fourteen. But that summer in 1997 was the first time I noted upon my cerebral jotter that money could buy you anything more worth having than a poxy bicycle. The Holy Grail of adolescence, the golden fleece of sexual awakening was almost within the clammy grasp of Nicholas and I – our moistened fingers were scrabbling at the edges – but we needed one thing badly in order to attain it. Privacy. And in order to get privacy, we needed money.

What I mean by this is that we thought a lot about different places we could do it. The obvious idea was a bedroom. But the question was, whose bedroom? I shared a bedroom with my fraternal millstone, whom I was most of the time able to intimidate into getting the fuck out, as I was forced to put it in language he could understand, when I wanted to crack one off. But he could definitely not be relied upon to be helpful. And this was too important an enterprise to leave to the whim of the same Neanderthal whelp who thought it the height of sophisticated humour to listen to my telephone conversations and mime blowjobs.

Plus, there were many other things about where I lived. We haven't really touched on my family yet, have we? I wonder how we've got this far without doing so. People like to talk about my family. They always have.

My father is, was, was and is, dead. He jumped off the bridge over the Piccadilly-to-Stalybridge line at approximately 8.56am on October 14th 1995. I know the approximate moment of death; not because I was with him at that moment, but because he managed to time his descent so that his airborne body collided precisely with the blunt nose of the 8.58 arrival into Oxford Road, just as it started the deceleration into the station. In the months following his death, I scrutinised carefully a number of trains making the same journey. Six times I took the train journey myself and noted the time when we passed the bridge. On innumerable other mornings I stood on the bridge, just where my father stood that autumn morning, and watched the train pass below until I saw it disappear into the curve of the station in the distance. I calculated that on average the train takes almost exactly two minutes from the moment that its front carriage passes the bridge until the moment when it arrives at the station. It follows that it was at approximately 8.56am that my father climbed on to the black, iron, birdshit-washed railings and let his body fall to meet the train. I have often wondered whether he engineered this collision on purpose. I am inclined to think that he did. He was a man of great exactitude.

My mother is… has been…was… insentient. In many ways. She is dead now too, but she wasn't *then*. Although she might as well have been. She came to life miraculously once a week to claim her various benefit cheques and to loyally patronise the local off-licence, and she had the odd psychotic episode during which she was animated to say the least, but other than that, she could reliably be found on the fetid couch behind closed curtains, doing a remarkable impression of a woodlouse.

My younger brother will, I fear, follow in the footsteps of my illustrious ex-stepfather, who is currently in prison for deeply unsavoury reasons. Not that I wish to hasten to malign the kettle, being something of a tarnished pot myself, but seriously, you don't want anything to do with that gentleman. I'm afraid that Jordan exhibited early signs of going the same way as his progenitor, and his behaviour over subsequent years has done little to disprove my suspicions. He is a disappointment to me. Not that I'm unsympathetic to the attempts of the young and hot-blooded to wriggle around a little in the straitjacket of this society of ours. One needs to do that just to work out how far is too far. But he's unimaginative. That's my problem. He steals what he's supposed to steal, and knocks about whoever he's supposed to knock about, and lies about things he's obviously the kind of person to lie about. He is, I regret to say, textbook.

The flat we lived in was one of those flats where the kitchen was the living room was the hall. It smelled of washing that had been left wet for too long, and of beer and fat and body odour. When Mum was having a bad one it smelled of sick.

So much for the Bradys. We have no lions on our gateposts. Thus, my family seat was unsuitable for our – my, Lizzie,

Rachel and Nick's – purposes in many respects, I'm sure you'll agree. So what other options were available to us?

Lizzie's bedroom? I beg to decline. The O'Leary abode was like an almighty man-trap for a youthful aspirant sexual pioneer such as myself. The brittle matriarch crouched around every corner, poised to spring upon the tiniest shred of evidence that Lizzie was a scarlet woman in the making, while her father cowered in a corner and whimpered. Lizzie, and I shit thee not here, was obliged to leave her bedroom door open whenever I came around. So much for that.

Nick and Rachel's houses presented more attractive prospects for the enterprise. Nick's parents were more disposed to let the precious cutting of their loins meander after the sun in his own sweet way. Have you met Stu and Gloria? They're precious. Chai-drinking, bruschetta-nibbling, fair-trade-brown-bag toting Guardianistas. Not that I didn't like them! Don't get that impression. I rather loved them actually, growing up. They doted on Nick so, and I found that both amusing and touching. But even more touching, actually, was how much he disappointed them, and how hard they kept trying to love him in spite of it. They wanted him to be brilliant, and innovative, and rebellious. And he was just nice and plodding and dull. Rachel thinks, I believe, that Nick's heroic mediocrity was some sort of gesture against this, the reverse battle of the kind that teenagers are supposed to have with their progenitors. I disagree. I think he strove to make them proud. He just couldn't manage it.

They had a series of naked pictures up. Expensive black and white things in frames. Three of them. Gloria naked, holding her round swollen stomach that was Nick. They were in the bedroom. Oh, poor Nick. The hell I gave him for those.

Sorry, that's irrelevant. All this is irrelevant, really. The point I'm trying to make is that they were generally very lenient. And, of course, minted. Nick had a big bedroom – not to be underestimated when you're thinking about choreographing four flailing bodies with a reasonable degree of comfort – and he had carte blanche to do whatever he liked – and he had a lock on the door. The lucky swine. It was the perfect set-up.

But – get this – he wouldn't let us use his room. When I put it to him, he just made a face like a disabled dog and said, *Dunno. It'd be weird. My parents an' all.*

Well, exactly – they'd love it, I retorted. *They'd probably join in if we asked them. Glory might lend me her nudey pics to get me started off.*

Shut up, you twat, he bleated, *we're not doing it at mine,* and loped off in a huff. And the next day he came, smug as you like, to tell us that his room was being redecorated over the next few weeks, so the option was out. Convenient, that.

So in the end, Rachel said we could do it at hers. It was a funny house, was Rachel's. Too big and too quiet for the two people in it. You could feel the dead mother, everywhere, still. Lots of photos. Lots of things that went a bit undone. They lived on frozen pizzas and the like. Not that I wasn't used to that, but my family lived on frozen pizzas because they were three for £4 from Iceland, whereas Rachel and her dad lived on them because the mother used to do the cooking and now she was gone. That's the impression I got, anyway. But Rachel's dad was out a lot, always during the day, and she had her own room – no lock on the door sadly, but you can't have it all. In fact, if we did it at Rachel's, we could actually have a room each. One for each couple, I mean. Lizzie and I would take Rachel's dad's bedroom, and Nick and Rachel would stay in Rachel's. I did feel that out of politeness I should offer Rachel the room with the double bed – after all, she was the hostess – but she was quite repulsed by the idea. *My dad's bed? That's gross.* So, that's how it was going to be.

In fact, we had an abortive trial run, and a most interesting little incident it was too. I think it set some of us on edge, though. After that, we realised that it just wasn't safe in our houses. And that was when I thought of the hotel.

Lizzie

She followed me. She knew where I was. She knew, she always knew. I don't know *how* she knew.

Rachel

Ah, yes. The trial run.

I had told my dad that I'd be going out that day, shopping in town with Lizzie. I don't know why I even bothered telling him that, it didn't achieve any purpose. I just felt the need to construct a story that was totally different from what I would actually be doing. Like, if he'd said, *What are you doing today?* and I'd said, *Oh, nothing much, just hanging around the house*, then it would have felt perilous, it would have felt like it was always on the tip of my tongue to say, *And I'm going to have sex, Dad. Today is the day I'm going to have sex.* But as it was, I said, *Lizzie and me are going shopping in town. I need some stuff from Paperchase and we might look in Miss Selfridge.* I had already bought some things, earlier that week, just in case he decided that evening that he cared what teenage girls bought these days and asked to see. I still remember – it was a notebook with zigzags in pink and purple on the cover, and some pens. And a top from Miss Selfridge, a flimsy thing made of netting that I didn't even like. In fact, that was part of my story; I was going to return it because I'd changed my mind. I'd also made up some background colour, that we'd bumped into some girls from school in town and had a chat with them, and that a guy got into a fight with ticket inspectors on the Metrolink 'cause he didn't have a ticket. I made up all these things, isn't that weird? Isn't it strange that I'd bother? I never usually told him about my day, so it would actually be pretty out of character for me to start now. But I didn't think of it like that. I just wanted to have this alternative day in my head, all filled out with events. Perhaps that says something about how I was feeling about the actual thing.

Dad seemed interested, actually, even though he was in the office that day so he wouldn't be around. He asked me what time I thought I'd be gone. Something about how somebody might come to check the boiler in the morning, so I should go out in the afternoon. Any time from one o'clock. Ha.

Nick

Yeah, I didn't want it to happen at my house. So what? I think I've got a right to decide that if I want. It just… I don't know, I just didn't like the thought of my parents being around. Which they always were. Plus, I was getting a bit pissed off at how Damien was trying to take the whole thing over. He did that with everything. And he thought he could dictate to me where we were going to do it. Well, sorry, mate, it doesn't quite work like that. Plus, I was having my room decorated at some point that summer, and Mum and Dad could have started to get the decorators in at any time. So it wasn't a good idea in any case.

He was always really disrespectful of my parents, you know. Damien, I mean. Especially my mum. He made these crude jokes about pictures of her up round the house. It's just a bit of a cheap shot, isn't it? 'Your mum' – oh very good, very original, quite the big ground-breaking comedian. It wasn't funny. It was just plain disrespectful. Because my parents were lovely to Damien. They gave him a lot. All the stuff his real mum didn't. They helped him out so much. And that was the way he repaid them. Pathetic.

The thing about me is, I get on great with my folks. Always have. They're proud of me, and I'm grateful to them. And Damien can't stand the simplicity of that. I suppose it's not that surprising, given his own home life.

Although, while we're on the subject of that, I wonder what

he's told you about his home life. It was never as bad as he made out, you know. I mean, obviously death's always really sad and everything, and there's no doubt his mum was basically a bad mother – should never have had kids in the first place. But he tends to ham it up a bit. I mean, for example, you know his dad didn't mean to kill himself? He was just pissed and stumbled through the barriers on a bit of the bridge they were repairing. The verdict at the inquest was accidental death – someone saw it happen. My dad told me. But Damien insists it was this great poetic act of suicide, a rejection of the world, a profound statement of some sort. He even seems to think his mum's problems were somehow glamorous, rather than…

Look, I know I probably sound really harsh right now. But I just hate the way he tries to paint himself as this great tragic hero, and as if everything that happened to him was the culmination of a massive operatic attempt by society to crush him. When really, society has been pretty good to him. He had a lot of opportunities. The flat they lived in was actually alright, you know – thanks very much, taxpayer. There were always people around to help him. Like, there was this teacher at school who was always really supportive, everyone knew he got special treatment. And then, like, Father Creevey. And my parents. And, sorry to say it, but maybe even me, and Lizzie. And the way he repaid us all was… well, you'll see.

Rachel
Essentially, what happened that Thursday was this.

They all came round to mine; we agreed to meet at two o'clock. I answered the door to Nick first. He came in and said, *Hi*, kind of shyly, and kissed me. I remember, he smelled, very strongly, of Lynx aftershave. That sounds pretty horrible but it was actually nice. I could tell, you know, that he'd made an effort. His hair was all gelled and he was wearing a stripey top that he knew I liked, and he just looked sort of clean and groomed, even more than usual. I had made an effort too. I hadn't eaten lunch 'cause I was too nervous. I had washed myself down below about five times, I kept thinking of problem pages I'd read in teen-girl magazines about how you might smell there and boys don't like it. I was always totally paranoid about that.

It's one of the great misconceptions you have as a teenage girl, actually. When I was in Japan, a few years ago, they used to have vending machines full of schoolgirls' used knickers in the train stations. Seriously.

We stood in the kitchen and kissed like strangers – he had to take his chewing gum out and put it in the bin first – and as we kissed I found myself shaking a bit. Then the door went and it was Lizzie and Day, they'd met down the road and come up together.

We all sat around in the living room, sort of not knowing how to get started. It felt weird and unreal, as if actually on some level we all knew it wasn't going to happen that day. I got us one of Dad's bottles of wine – he had loads in the cupboard. It was red. I opened it and poured us all a glass in the special wine glasses. We all sat on the sofas and drank it politely, but it all felt a bit, I don't know, ridiculous, and I could feel myself blushing. It was as if I admitted I needed the drink. No, it wasn't that. It was the fact it was wine. Too high-flown. We should have had cheap beer or something.

Anyway, we chatted a bit, about this and that, school and stuff, and eventually Day laughed and said, *Come on then, action stations*, and took Lizzie by the hand and started climbing up the stairs. I looked at Nick and he looked at me and we followed them. Day and Lizzie went into Dad's room and Nick and I into mine. I caught both their eyes quickly, Lizzie's and Day's, as I closed the door. Day looked amused. Lizzie – well, I don't know.

So, Nick and I were in there, in my room. We hadn't been in there yet. He hadn't even met my dad. We usually hung out at his, where like I told you, I always expected he'd want to do stuff, but he didn't, not really, just the odd snog. We hadn't really done *anything* yet.

So, this was it. We kissed, he looped his arms round my waist and put his hands on my bum, and I could feel something, not exactly hard but just that there was something there. The word *erection* popped into my head, in a pompous voice like from a biology textbook or something, and the thought occurred to me that I hadn't even seen him naked yet and now we were going to have sex, and I started laughing and couldn't stop. He said, *What, what?* He didn't like people laughing at him, still doesn't. No matter who it is or why. So I said, *Nothing*, and I thought of Day and the priest, and so I kissed him again and started undoing his trousers, or trying to. And a few minutes passed. And then I heard creaking on the stairs and a woman's voice call outside, *Michael?*

We jumped out of our skins — I stumbled back from Nick and stared at the door and he scrabbled to do his fly up and hissed, *Who's that?*

I don't know! I said, and because it was all I could do, I smoothed my hair and checked my clothes and then I opened the door and went out on to the landing.

Lizzie's mum was walking up the stairs. She stopped dead and looked at me. I thought she'd come for Lizzie. I was shaking, but I tried to stay calm and said, *Hi, Mrs. O'Leary*. She looked at me and didn't say anything, and I thought, *Where are Day and Lizzie, what are they doing, shall I say they're here or shall I pretend they're not?* And then a bit of me thought, *She can't go in my dad's room! She's not even in her own house! It's my house!* And I said, *Can I help you?* She said, *Rachel, I didn't...* and then the door opened and Lizzie and Day came out. Lizzie looked at her mum and her mum looked at Lizzie and then said to her very quietly, *What are you doing here?* I sensed that Nick had walked out behind me and I realised how it looked. It looked exactly like it was. Lizzie said, *Nothing,* even more quietly, so quietly that if I hadn't seen her lips move I wouldn't have known she spoke. Her mum said, *I don't believe you. Come home, now.* And at that moment I realised what emotion I had seen on her face a moment before, what it was that had been wiped out and replaced by triumph when she saw Lizzie and Day. My ears filled up with noise because then I *knew,* and I said, *What are you doing here?*

And that was when Dad came home.

Michel

Of course I knew what they were up to. Give me a little credit. I knew something was going on, just from the way that Rachel recited a detailed description of her plans for the day before I went to work, exactly as if she'd learned it off by heart. It was unlike her. I didn't know exactly what she was planning, I thought she might be going to get drunk in the park or something – that's what parents always seem to be terrified of in England. But, though it might seem naive, I didn't think she would be at home. I don't know why. I just naturally equated teenage mischief with being somewhere else – not in the house where you watch television with your father. That's how it was when I was young. Which is why I made the plans that I did.

When I walked into the house, I passed through the living room and I saw the wine bottle and the glasses on the coffee table. I would have stood there looking at them and thinking for longer, except that I heard Rachel upstairs, saying, *What are you doing here?* At first I thought she was talking to me, but then I suddenly became aware that Kathleen was standing on the stairs, and that there were quite a lot of people in my house who had no official business being there.

I crossed over to the stairs and saw Kathleen, who looked down at me and said, *Michael I'm not quite sure what's going on here.* I looked up and saw the children and thought, *Ah.* That was it.

Kathleen

I remember the day that Rachel and her father moved in. That house had been empty for a while. It had been an old couple – the Walshes – living there, and one of them had died and the other gone into a nursing home. I could just about see the driveway from our window, and one day I saw the removal van parked outside, and men unloading things. I watched them for a while. I saw the little girl standing around reading a book. Just standing up, reading. It was funny. I'd never seen that before, looked kind of as if she was sleepwalking.

I assumed it was a family who were moving in. So I went over to say hello, and brought Lizzie with me. She wasn't at school so it must have been the holidays.

He answered the door. He was older than I'd expected. He had grey hair. I can't remember exactly what I said to him exactly, something about wanting to welcome him and his family to the neighbourhood. He told me that he didn't have a wife. He was French, he had a strong accent, although his English was pretty good. I had never met a Frenchman before. My head was full of stereotypes, men from old films in berets with curly moustaches. But he was clean shaven.

I didn't know what to say, about the wife I mean, until he said that he was a widower. And then I knew at least to say sorry.

He said his name was Michel, and the way he said it I heard it wrong, and repeated it like Michelle. He laughed and said I could call him Michael if that was easier, it was the same name really, he said. So I did.

Alright, I can't lie. I was struck by how good-looking he was, that first time I met him. You couldn't not be. Ask anyone. But it was sort of a sleazy good-looking. Too dark and brooding to be taken seriously. The accent didn't help with that impression either. So I thought, *Oho, I bet I know your game.* And I resolved to have a good old laugh at the single women trying to snare him. Susie Busnell at Number Seventeen, and poor old Margaret Moss. A single Frenchman in our midst! A sitting duck. I marked him out as interesting, I grant you, but I never considered myself in danger at all.

He made a big effort to fit in. He was Catholic and everything, so that helped. He came to church on Sundays and sent Rachel to confirmation classes. He donated things for the Harvest Collection and the Christmas Fair. He joined the Catenians, which was the mens' club Paul was a member of, for Catholic businessmen. Paul liked him. *Clever bloke,* he'd say. *He knows what's what.*

He was just a neighbour, you know, at the beginning. But a nice neighbour. An interesting one. I thought Lizzie and Rachel might be friends, at first — I was always trying to get her to make friends with nice girls. But they took a big dislike to each other. Or rather, Lizzie would never make an effort with Rachel. Sometimes I'd see him, Michael, in the street doing his garden, or we'd talk after mass, and we'd push the two girls off together, to play. Lizzie would just stand there with her lip out, grouching. I said to her once, *Why don't you ever go over and play with that nice Rachel Vincent on the weekend? Or have her round here for tea. We'll do party tea.*

She's silly, she said.

What d'you mean, silly? I asked her.

She talks funny.

That's because she's from France, silly, I said. *Her English is very good. It's better than your French.*

She's always reading. She's boring, she'd say. And then it'd always be, *Can I go and play with Day?*

Always him, wasn't it, you see? Even then. Always the boys.

Look, I was interested in him. I had no intention of anything. But he sort of… he was interested too. In me. I wonder, do you know how lonely it can get, being married to someone like Paul? I had kind of been sleepwalking, for all those years, stuck in this life as a wife, as a mother. A parishioner. Do you know how old I was at this point?

Michael worked from home a lot. I stayed at home too, obviously. We'd see each other sometimes in the road, popping out to the corner shop for some milk or a newspaper, or getting into the car to do some errands. We'd stop and chat. Once, he invited me in for a cuppa and a biscuit. And soon it became a habit that we'd have a cuppa in the middle of the day – tea for me, and coffee for him – just to have a chat. About what we were doing at the moment, about the kids, about people in the parish. Such silly, frivolous chat we had in those first few weeks I knew him, when I look back on it. Chat that meant nothing at all. But to me, in my life… it felt like… the feeling when you're walking after a hard frosty winter and you see daffodils. Glad.

It was a funny house, the one he and Rachel lived in. Well, not really the house itself, more how it was furnished. Not really a home as I was used to thinking of it. Nothing matched. It was full of slightly odd bits of china and dark varnished wood furniture, alongside crappy bits of Ikea stuff that hadn't been properly assembled. It looked temporary. I know this is a cliché, but it really needed a woman's touch. I couldn't help myself occasionally rearranging things, fixing things. Wiping the dust off the mantelpiece with a tissue. Bringing him some flowers to brighten the place up.

He was from Brittany, this bit of France I'd never really heard of. That's where all the odd antique bits came from, the cuckoo clock and the bellows and the varnished pottery plates with pictures of flowers on them. His parents' house there. He was always talking about this Brittany. Said it was like a little corner of the world frozen in time. Full of beaches of long grey shivering sand, and market towns full of old ladies wearing stiff dark Breton dress. *You would love it, I think,* he said. *It is difficult to love, but once you do love it, you never love anywhere else.* He asked where I was from. And he asked me about where I grew up, the farm and the village and that. He said we were both Celts at heart. We used to sit there until late morning became afternoon, talking about our younger days, revisiting these little wild bits of country where we grew up.

He never talked about his first wife. Not in those days. Whenever he left the room, to get a fresh pot of coffee or to go to the lav or whatnot, I looked at the pictures of her that were up on the mantelpiece. She was pretty enough. I felt strange when I looked at them, him younger, dark haired, slimmer, laughing. I tried to picture them together, the younger him and this pretty ghost, animated to life from the pictures. I became obsessed with thinking about them.

Sometimes, unwanted, the image was me and him instead. Younger, somewhere else. On a beach, in this Brittany.

He saw me looking at the pictures, one time, when he came back into the room quietly. The next time I came around, they weren't there.

But, the thing is, after that, when I dropped around out of the blue to collect something I'd forgotten, they were back up. So I knew, he just took them down for me.

I once heard someone say that the definition of temptation is the split second between the moment when it's too early to struggle and the moment when it's too late to struggle. Implying, you know, that temptation doesn't really exist. That you can't help falling.

It was one rainy, completely normal day in March that it happened. I made the tea, and I scalded my hand with some boiling water from the kettle by mistake. A stupid mistake. He held my hand under the cold tap for a long time, too long. He held it and held it, and his fingers pushed through mine like the straws of a basket weave. And that was it.

Rachel

Dad managed to make it all normal. He said hello to everyone and said, *Kathleen, you came for the book I assume?* And she said, *Yes – Lizzie, you'll be coming home now, you've got things to do*, and then the two of them, Dad and Lizzie's mum, looked at each other and went downstairs and the four of us stood there and didn't dare to look at each other for a few seconds. Then Lizzie started snivelling a bit and Nick said, *I'm gonna go.* They walked down the stairs – Lizzie ran, Nick walked – and Day followed them. He grinned at me as he left. I got the feeling he was enjoying himself.

I went to my room, and I cried for the first time since Mum died. I wasn't crying for us, though. I was crying because I knew what Lizzie's mum was doing in our house in the middle of the day, and I suddenly felt that it was all too big for me. Too big and too much.

Lizzie

I ran home and sat in my room. Dad wasn't at home. I sat in my room and waited for her to come.

She came in eventually. She came up the stairs, and stood in the doorway with her arms folded. I could tell her arms were folded just from the way she was breathing. I wasn't looking at her. I was looking at a stained bit of the carpet that was a slightly different colour to the rest of it. I was making my eye go round it tracing the edges of the different coloured patch. As long as I traced the shape perfectly, she wouldn't start speaking.

I must have got it wrong eventually, because she was like, *What were you doing with that boy?*

I said, *Nothing.* I realised at that moment that he still had my knickers. He'd just taken them off and put his mouth on the inside of my thigh when we heard the noise, and they were still in his hand. He must have taken them. But then I thought, *Oh God, what if they're still there?* I tipped my head forward so my hair fell like all over my face, because I knew I'd blush, and because I just wanted to hide.

She was like, *Did you sleep with him, you stupid girl?*

No! I said.

She said, *I don't believe you,* and I said, *I know, you never believe me,* and she was like, *Don't be so bloody cheeky.* Then she came and got my wrists and gripped them tightly, and was like, *Lizzie, do not give yourself away like a packet of Bacardi Breezers.* I said, *Bacardi Breezers don't come in packets.* She was like, *Shut up. I'm telling you this for your own good.* Then she slapped me on the face.

I started crying as loud as I could, 'cause that was the only thing that ever stopped her, 'cause she was scared somebody would think we weren't a happy family or whatever. She was like, *I'm telling you this for your own good! Don't you think I don't love you?* Then she started crying too. She wiped her face and got up and was like, *What have I done to deserve such a daughter?*

I said, *I wish I wasn't your daughter.* But I lay down and said it into my pillow

What? she said, and stopped in the doorway.

How did you know where I was? I pretended I'd said. But she didn't answer.

Michel

I don't know why. Because she was a beautiful woman. Because it had been two years. Because she wanted me. Because I was lonely. All the clichés. Insert your own cliché here. You might as well.

Actually, the greatest cliché is *I was lonely in the evenings,* isn't it? *The nights were so cold,* as the songs go. That wasn't the case for me. I had my daughter. We sat and watched the television and I tried to tell her things. So, the evenings were not the problem. It was a different kind of loneliness. A blankness in my chest, a pain of absence, that could come to get me at the times that I would least expect. During the middle of the day when I checked my answerphone messages. While I brushed my teeth in the morning and saw that my gums were receding like my mother's. In the car. In a traffic jam, when I put a polo in my mouth and thought of minty breath. A sort of empty misery that only having her body on mine could dispel. So I'd do it again. And then I would be alright for a little while longer.

I never got that empty feeling when I was with Rachel. But Rachel was starting to have her own life, her own secrets. She was not around as much in the evenings as she used to be.

That is no excuse, is it?

Of course, it was a terrible idea. It was a terrible thing to do. Paul. The children. I didn't even like her. I wanted her. I didn't *like* her.

Does that make you think I'm a bad person? I suppose that I liked her at first, a bit. We were friends, in a way. We used to sit and have coffee together, and talk. But she mainly talked about her husband, about how stupid or dull he was. Not straight out, of course – it was just a little joke about him here and there. Then she would roll her eyes. Then the jokes became snipes. And finally long, bitter conversations. About Lizzie, too. Her daughter. She wanted Lizzie to be like Rachel.

I felt so sorry for her. Because you can usually tell a lot from the way that people treat those nearest to them about how they treat themselves. You are hardest on the people who reflect yourself back at you. Kathleen hated Paul because she feared that she, like him, was dull. She bullied Lizzie because she saw herself in Lizzie's compulsive flirting, her love of men. She hadn't figured this out of course. She was younger than me. Much younger. Almost a child herself.

Yes, I felt sorry for her. But I didn't like her.

It was very clear to me, the whole time, why she was there. She carried herself a certain way around me. She touched my possessions with a peculiar intensity. She asked me, with forensic diligence, about my past. Which, I cannot lie, is very flattering.

She touched my arm when we met and my shoulder when we parted, and when I passed her tea her fingers would brush the skin of my hand.

Yes, I wanted her. But I didn't like her.

That day, the day that Rachel found out, I lost my moral authority over my daughter. I resigned it for good. There was nothing I could do except sit back and watch things happen.

Kathleen

I tried to stop it. Of course I did. After that first time, the cold day in March when I scalded my hand, I told him I couldn't see him any more. I went home and prayed. I was too ashamed, too disgusted with myself, to even go to confession. Some things are too bad to confess.

I tried to avoid him. But he pursued me. Honest to God, I have never been pursued like that before. Before I was married, or since, or after. He followed me. He made any excuse to see me. Everywhere I went, I could feel his eyes sort of boring into me. I was going mad. Crazy. I couldn't concentrate.

I just went around there to tell him to leave me alone. I had worked out a whole speech, a talk that would cleanse all these feelings in my head and my heart and leave me just… as I was before. Not happy, I'd never been happy. But okay. Content.

I started my speech, but he started to kiss my cheeks, my chin, my earlobe. He was kissing each freckle, he told me later.

Well, that was it.

And then, God forgive me, I was happy.

Day

A minor setback. A bagatelle! Nothing to speak of, for a team such as we, a quartet of such verve and resolve. But as I've already said, this incident made it clear to us that, if nothing else, our houses could no longer be considered as potential locations for the mighty enterprise. We had to find another solution.

We considered everything. We had a nice run of weather for a few days, and we thought about going down to the Bollin in Altrincham, where there was babbling water and tall waving grass, and only a token amount of empty Fosters cans and dog shit. But Rachel said she'd read a *Cringe! Embarrassing Stories!* thing once in a magazine about a girl who'd done it outside in a field, and a dog came up and licked her tit halfway through and she didn't fancy *that*, thanks very much – and then it started being rainy again. We wondered briefly if there was a chance of getting invited to a house party with a surplus of empty rooms and a deficit of watchful parents, but, well, nothing appropriate came along and we were impatient. And then it hit me. We should go to a hotel.

They wouldn't let us, Nick bleated when I put it to him. *We're too young.*

We'll work something out, I said

It'll cost money, he objected.

We'll find the money, I soothed.

Where?

I pretended to think really hard.

Rachel

The funny thing is, it didn't put us off at all. I mean, don't get me wrong, I think all of us were a bit shaken in different ways. Apart from Day. Lizzie was upset because her mum had had a go at her even more than usual – even more of a go than we imagined, as it turned out. And I was upset because I knew Lizzie's mum was fucking my dad, which was something I think it's fair enough to be a bit upset about. Out of all of us, I think maybe Nick was most shaken, though. He always had a, sort of, fear of doing wrong, you know. A real instinct for not getting into trouble. He was always a model citizen in the making. I knew this from the first evening when we sat watching that film, side by side, politely dipping our hands in turn into the bowl of popcorn. And you know the funny thing? It was such a bore for his parents, who would have simply loved a rebellious son with whom they could *empathise*. They were always baffled at his consistent failure to shock them. Poor old Nick.

Although, I suppose maybe you could say he's one step ahead of the rest of us here. Maybe he had figured out that the only way to disappoint his parents was not to disappoint them. That the only way he could actually genuinely rebel against them was by consistently refusing to rebel. That was why he started putting the brakes on when it looked as though we might get caught. Not that he was scared of punishment, like Lizzie for example – and boy, did she get punished. Because he didn't want to give Stu and Gloria the satisfaction.

Either way, I think he would have been quite happy to just let the whole thing slide, if Day hadn't kept on at him about it, which was always the surest way to get him to do something. Same with Day, incidentally, you could make him want something most by telling him Nick had it. You might have noticed this already.

But I think it's fair to say that Lizzie and I both got *more* into the idea after that incident. Personally, I just couldn't think of anything that would make me happier than to have really pissed off her mum. And my sense of responsibility to my dad had just gone out of the window, ever since I knew he was carrying on with her. I thought about it all the time, from then on.

Dad didn't speak to me about the incident in the house, by the way. I came downstairs that afternoon, after my eyes had finally gone back to normal and I felt I could face him. I wanted to tell him how angry I was, how horrible that woman was, how it was an insult to my mum. How *tacky* it all was. I had all this stuff planned out in my head, I'd been practising upstairs.

Then, when I passed the kitchen, I saw that the wine bottle was in the bin and the four wine glasses had been washed up and were drying upside down in the washing-up rack. I stood and looked at them for a bit, and tried to figure out what to do.

Then I went to the living room and peeped around the door. He didn't look up from his paper.

Has she gone then? I said, and my voice was all trembly.

Yes, he said. *Your friends have gone too.*

I see how it is! I said.

He put his paper down. He looked at me and opened his mouth. Then he closed it again and picked the paper up. *If you want wine, you can just ask me for it,* he said.

That was it. That was all he ever said on the matter. I knew that he knew, and he knew that I knew that he knew. But *he* also knew that *I* knew.

It was checkmate, I suppose, of a sort.

Kathleen

And so it carried on. I know exactly how long it carried on for. Two years and five months and seventeen days.

Are you speaking to him now? When did you last see him? I know he'll say he didn't love me, because that makes it easier for him. That's how you can *tell* it was important to him. I'll tell you something, I have never met anybody so messed up as that man in my life. His wife's death… it just destroyed him. We'd talk about it when he lay in my arms and he would cry like a baby. He was so frightened of loving again, of losing the person he loved again. He would push me away, then pull me back. Push, then pull. What chance did I stand?

When I called things off – *I* called things off more than once, I bet he didn't tell you that – he wouldn't leave me alone. He'd come by the house during the day, he'd call the house phone incessantly so I had to take it off the hook because Lizzie got suspicious. He wrote me letters. Dozens of letters. I've still got them, you know. Do you want to see them? Put them in this little file, this, this investigation you seem to be doing? He wouldn't like that at all. Bet those letters wouldn't tally with the story he's been telling you. Not at all.

But it was my fault in the end. I'd go back to him, I'd always go back in the end. And then he'd get scared again and go distant on me and say, *I'm confused, I'm confused.* Push, pull, push, pull. It was like a bloody tug of war. Only one person could win. It was never going to be me, was it? I'd lost from the very beginning, when I first gave in to him.

I was stupid. I believed him when he said he loved me, so I decided to leave Paul. It's not like I enjoyed it… the affair, you know, the secrecy of it. I hated it! I struggled with myself and I went through hell and I decided eventually that, although it went against everything I believed, it was the only way. I'd leave Paul and I'd go to Michael. I'd divorce Paul and I'd marry Michael. The lie would be over.

And then I met him on a Saturday night, *that* Saturday night, and he told me he didn't want me anymore.

Rachel

From then on, the boys thought they were doing all the preparation with all their little phone calls in the park, but there was one thing they hadn't even thought about. Can you guess what it was? And, to be fair, neither had Lizzie and I. Not until after the trial run. Thought about it, I mean. She brought it up with me one day afterwards, and I thought, *Bloody hell, yeah, I hadn't even thought about that.*

I mean, I'd probably still have done it, if my mum hadn't turned up, she said.

I was shocked, I guess. I said, *You don't want to get pregnant, do you?*

Dunno, she said, *There's not much else for me to do is there? I'm not, like,* academic, *like all the rest of you.*

I looked over to see if she was having a laugh. She looked perfectly serious and I said, *For real, Lizzie, that's not a good idea.*

Then she said, *I know, I'm joking. God.*

I don't know, though. I don't know if she was.

So we decided to go to the Brook Clinic just near Mosley Street in town. It was the first time really that we'd done anything together, just the two of us. We didn't want the boys to come. We didn't even tell them.

I laid all my clothes out on the bed that morning and looked at them with great dissatisfaction. It seemed important what to wear that day. Even more important than what to wear for doing the thing itself – perhaps, I guess, because we wouldn't be wearing much for that at all, ultimately. I chose a lilac blouse and blue suede trousers, horrible things I never normally wore. The blouse was too tight and peeped open between the buttons, and the trousers were uncomfortable. But at least it was a *serious* outfit. It felt like a disguise.

We went, and we were sitting in the waiting room, and I looked round at all the other girls there. They were all young. They were all fatter than they should have been, spilling out of too-tight tops and waistbands. They slouched, and stared into the distance, and picked their spots, and blew bubbles. There was one with two kids playing on the floor. As I watched her she started scratching her crotch. I looked away, and wondered how old she was. There were no boyfriends.

I wondered what they thought of us. I looked sideways at Lizzie sitting next to me, drawing everyone's gazes. Like she always did.

The nurse agreed to see us together. She was nice, I suppose. Asked us a load of questions, took our blood pressure and prescribed us a clever little shiny green pack full of yellow pills, and gave us each a paper bag stuffed with condoms in foil red and blue packets. They looked like sweets or something. It was all very colourful. For a mad moment, I thought about party bags.

The nurse looked over at Lizzie as she wrote out the prescription. *That's a nasty bruise,* she said. Lizzie followed the nurse's eyes to her forearm, and mine did too, and I noticed that yeah, she had a bruise on the inside of her arm, a little nearer her wrist than her elbow. All purple and yellow coloured. She usually kept her sleeves pulled over her hands, it was kind of a habit I suppose, so I hadn't noticed. *Yeah,* Lizzie said, *Dunno how I did that.* The nurse looked at her but didn't say anything.

I thought, *Day? No.*

And then I realised. Her mum.

Lizzie suggested we go to get a Frappuccino at Starbucks, which was the height of sophistication for us in those days. I ordered the raspberry one. Lizzie got chocolate. We sat at the little ledge by the window, and watched the people and the rain outside the window.

I hate that kind of thing, Lizzie said. *Don't you?*

What kind of thing? I said.

Being asked all those questions and that. Having to tell them about stuff you've done, you know?

You mean the sex stuff? I said.

Yeah, it's a bit embarrassing, I suppose, I said. I didn't mind, though. Not really. Maybe because I hadn't actually done anything. So when the nurse had asked I could just say, *Nope, nope, nope.* Lizzie had said *yes* to oral sex, blushing prettily. I was mildly intrigued, but it didn't surprise me. I couldn't imagine getting to the end of a film with Day without being touched.

I just know they're always judging you, she said. *Everyone is. Even that nurse was. But she doesn't know the whole story.*

What d'you mean?

Well, it's not like I'm a slut, you know? she said. *I'm not like Hilary Dawson or whatever. You know, she'll do anything with anyone. She'll, like, give all these guys a blowjob who she doesn't even like.*

Really? I said. *Who told you that?*

Everyone knows it, come on, Lizzie said, and rolled her eyes.

I guess so, I said.

Anyway, it's not like that with me, you know? It's just him. I'd only ever do it with him. I hate the idea of people thinking I'm like Hilary Dawson.

I stirred the cream on my Frappuccino. I didn't know how to respond to all this. I thought about changing the subject, to ask her about her bruise, but didn't know how. I was staring at it, I suppose. She saw me and pulled her sleeves down around her wrists. Then she finished her drink and said, *I'm done.*

So I never asked her.

That makes me sound selfish, doesn't it? I should have cared more. Realised it might have been important. Maybe I was selfish. Kids are, generally. But she also has this way, Lizzie does, of shutting you up before you've even asked. I guess I also didn't ask because I knew she wouldn't tell me.

Anyway, she bruised easily. Whenever she bumped into a chair or fell off a bike she'd blossom up in massive purple bruises. That delicate skin and all.

Karen Cox

I don't remember the booking, to be honest with you. I don't even know if it was me what took it. D'you know how long ago you're talking? I'm not being funny, but a lot happens in fifteen years. I'm not exactly going to remember one specific phone call, even if it did turn out to be quite important in the end.

Don't get me wrong, I remember the thing itself. Bloody hell, the press we had over that. We had police and all sorts of other people round giving us a bit of that for months, didn't we? I said to them, I said, *Look, what more could we have done? How were we supposed to know what they was up to?* They had this story about the house being redecorated, and their dad and all. And they were pretty big lads, didn't look fourteen. Plus we never saw nothing of the girls. So how were we supposed to know what was going on? They said, *You shouldn't take cash without ID.* And I nodded and said, *I can only apologise. Terrible mistake. Never happened before, and it won't happen again.* And I thought in my head, at the same time, *Show me the owner of one small business that doesn't take cash without ID and I'll show you a liar.*

Needless to say, when we figured out what had happened and found the keys, we took all the proper precautions. Can't fault us there.

Nick

I had about sixty quid saved up, which I figured out was probably enough, so I said we could use it. Damien didn't offer to contribute, naturally. Yeah, I know he couldn't afford it and everything. Cry me a river. So, we were looking for a hotel that came in at under sixty quid for a twin room, for a Saturday night, that didn't require a credit card to make a booking. Harder to find than you might expect, actually. But we did it in the end. Spent hours in the park, on the phone.

We'd made up this story. Damien pretended to be our dad – oh yes, of course he had to be the one who made the call; I just sat back and let him get on with it while he did some ridiculous booming falsetto. He said he wanted to book a hotel room for the night because his house was being renovated. When they asked for the credit card details, he said he had just had his credit card stolen but would send his two sons around with the money later that day to pay for the room.

When we saw the place, to be honest I remember wondering why we bothered coming up with this elaborate story at all. Total dive. They clearly didn't give a crap about credit cards, dads or anything else. In fact, I'm amazed they cared enough to chase us up afterwards when they found the keys.

It's funny that we didn't expect the girls to contribute. Rachel asked me what we were doing about money at one point, but of course I told her not to worry about it. She didn't seem happy. She was a bit funny like that. Independent.

Of course, I didn't tell her it was just me footing the bill. I let her think me and Damien were splitting it. So maybe that made her feel a bit better about not paying.

What a mug.

Day

We made the calls in the park. We couldn't afford to be overheard, you see. Well, I say *we* made the calls – actually, *I* was the one who made the calls, because my voice had broken. Poor Nick still tended to err a little on the squeaky side, and we couldn't have that, seeing as I was impersonating my own father. Well, mine and Nick's father, for the purposes of the story we'd made up. Brothers, us! Imagine.

Father Patrick Creevey

How are you getting along there?

Don't mind me, just thought I'd pop in and see how it was going. Have you figured out what happened yet? I hope they're not all terribly upset. Young Rachel in particular has a tendency to get very upset about all this, when it comes up. Aggressive, almost. She's a modern girl in every sense of the word, you know. Quite a lot of front, very sure of herself, even a bit bolshy. But one can't help feeling, can one, that underneath all that, she's rather lost?

Let me ask you something. Do you really think it's a good idea to bring it all up again now? I mean that as an honest question, I have no agenda. Who are you trying to help? What good will it do? Or are you just, you know, interested?

If the latter, might I ask you *why?* I mean no offence, and I hope you'll take none, but we should all interrogate ourselves, you know, as well as others. Why are you here?

Oh, I daresay you might feel by now rather as if you're not asking the questions any more. Everybody is just telling you whatever the heck they like, by now. I know that feeling, I can tell you! *Bless me, Father, for I have sinned,* often in practice means *You know why I've always hated my sister?* or, *Twenty ways in which my dad ruined my life.* Be patient, though. The circuitous route is often the most diverting, as well as the least dangerous. They'll get there in the end.

Rachel will have a lot to tell you, I'm sure. Maybe the most, out of them all. She has a lovely speaking voice, doesn't she? A voice made for the radio, I always thought. Yes, I think it's her who was the most upset by all this in the long run, at least that's how I remember it. Not that I see her around here much anymore – she lives in London now, I've heard. But she comes back occasionally. To see a special someone I think... though that's mere idle gossip. I'm getting to be a bit of a gossip in my old age, I confess. I must watch myself.

Nicholas Gardner lives here again now. He comes to church with his wife – such a nice young couple! We need more like them in the parish. He seems perfectly undamaged. By this whole business, I mean. Although it was him, of course, who came to me the night before they did it. As well as afterwards, when he wanted to talk about... well, anyway. He seems very happy these days, unlike some. Rather bolsters up my theory, doesn't it, that confession helps one to be well adjusted in the long run?

I still see Damien Brady around. He wants to talk about this whole incident a lot – one kind of gets the feeling he rather enjoys it. He likes to shock people. Strange. Or maybe not so strange. You decide.

Lizzie O'Leary? I don't think anyone has seen her for years. You hear the odd thing, but no idea if it's true.

Well. I'll leave you to it.

Oh – just one last question. What do you think happened? So far, I mean. What do you believe?

Rachel
Get this.

We believe in one God, the Father, the Almighty, Maker of Heaven and Earth, of all that is Seen and Unseen. We believe in one Lord, Jesus Christ, only Son of God, eternally begotten of the Father, God from God, Light from Light, True God from True God. Begotten not made, of one Being with the Father,

Through Him all Things were made, for us Men and for our Salvation, He came down from Heaven, By the Power of the Holy Spirit, He became incarnate from the Virgin Mary, and was made Man. For our sake, He was crucified under Pontius Pilate, He suffered Death and was buried. On the third Day He rose again, in accordance with the Scriptures. He ascended into Heaven and is seated at the Right Hand of the Father. He will come again in Glory to judge the Living and the Dead, and His Kingdom will have no End. We believe in the Holy Spirit, the Lord, the Giver of Life, who proceeds from the Father and the Son, with the Father and the Son He is worshipped and glorified. He has spoken through the Prophets. We believe in one Holy, Catholic and Apostolic Church. We acknowledge one Baptism for the forgiveness of Sins. We look to the resurrection of the Dead, and THE LIFE OF THE WORLD TO COME, AMEN.

I know, right?

Day

So, we found a place that would take our booking a few days beforehand. *I* found a place. It was called the Brooklands Best Bed and Breakfast, which should give you an idea of what it was like. Not exactly the Ritz on the Champs-Élysées, I freely admit. A tottering terraced house that smelled of rancid bacon fat and cigarette smoke. Peeling walls and mouldering pot pourri, you know the type of thing. But the important things about the Brooklands Best Bed and Breakfast were that it was ideally located – far enough from the Close to make it reasonably safe, but near enough to facilitate our initial investigations – and that it cost fifty-five pounds for a twin room for a Saturday night. And, of course, that there were vacancies. Oh, there were vacancies! Between you and I, when I think of it now I find it hard to believe that they didn't know exactly what the score was from the very beginning. But there were such vacancies. And we paid cash.

We made the booking by phone, and then we, Nick and I, went by to pay in cash, on the Thursday before the Saturday of the great Games themselves. There was nobody at the reception desk – a fortuitous sign, I felt. A radio was blaring out the eerily cheerful tones of Key 103. I looked around for a bell to rap smartly, but no such thing existed, so we hallooed until a formidable woman with expansive red tresses waddled in and asked what we wanted in a tone indicative of some irritation. *We're here to pay for a room, our papa telephoned you yesterday, ma'am,* we chorused like cherubim. She took our cash and made a note in the book, and then, as planned, I made a series of detailed enquiries about the breakfast options available while Nick feigned embarrassed boredom and started wandering off looking at the tired prints on the wall, inspecting the scuffed skirting boards, peering into the breakfast area, gradually wandering further and further, scouting out the terrain. I grant it him, he did a marvellous job, came back later with a detailed description. Of the back door (propped open – it was hot weather). The wall. The position of the fire alarms.

I was somewhat nervous if you can credit it, since suspicion at this time would have consigned all our plans to ruin. I'm afraid that the only thing that I seemed to be able to think about was eggs. And so I blathered away – *I like my eggs poached, but softly poached you understand, with a creamy coating of mucus; it mingles so deliciously with the hollandaise sauce. Speaking of which, might one enquire if the hollandaise sauce is piquant in this establishment? I do so hate a bland hollandaise sauce* – while the redoubtable dame gazed upon me with an expression of stupefied incomprehension. Then Nick reappeared, and I rounded off my culinary enquiries with a flourish, and we departed.

Eggs. But it did the job, didn't it?

Rachel

I know Nick went to confession the night before we did it. I know that because he told me so. Years later. I don't know, maybe five, six years later. Something like that. One of the times when he rang me up.

He had this stage, you see, some years after it happened, of calling me at three o'clock in the morning, every six months. Almost exactly once every six months. He was always drunk. The funny thing was – well, it would have been funny if it wasn't so sad – he always pretended at first that he hadn't meant to call me. My phone would go in the middle of the night, and I'd wake up and reach out and pick it up and say, *Hello?* not really knowing what I was doing 'cause I was still half asleep, and he'd say, *Hello?* in a surprised sort of way, as if I'd just rung *him*. And then I'd say, *Nick, is that you?* And he'd say, *Who is this?* And it'd go on that way for quite a while. Eventually he'd admit that he'd called me, and then after a bit of pissed chitchat he'd always want to talk about what happened that summer. *Our first time*, he always called it. And, one of those times, he told me that he went to confession the night before, and told Father Patrick that we were going to do it.

Now, I suppose I can understand that in a way. But if I had gone to confession the night before, I would have meant it like sticking two fingers up. But I think Nick really wanted to tell the priest, just for the sake of telling him. He had cold feet. I've told you something about how Nick is with breaking the rules, so it's not actually that surprising. In fact, the only surprising thing is that he still went ahead with it the next day. That we actually ended up doing it at all.

Me? I spent the evening before with my dad. He sometimes had a go at cooking quite ambitious things, when the mood took him. Usually he was more of a frozen meals kind of guy, but occasionally he just decided, off the cuff, to cook something big, and flailed around in the kitchen making a mess, and then never used the ingredients again so they clogged up the cupboards till I threw them out. That evening I came home to find him cooking beef bourguignon, which was a frankly bizarre decision, given the sweltering weather. But I ate it and said it was very nice. Then we watched TV together. I felt like it was tense between us but couldn't tell how far that was just my own nerves. We had been to the arcade that day, and in the evening I noticed that my dad grips his wine glass like a joystick. When he says something and he means it to be important, he tilts it forward or back a bit.

I love my dad. But I wasn't really in the mood to listen to what he had to say that evening. I went to bed early.

Nick

Who told you that? I mean, I don't really remember. Look, that's a bit of a personal question to ask in any case, isn't it? I mean, I'm happy to talk about this to an extent, I don't really get why you're that bothered but whatever, why not? But there's a reason why confession stays private isn't there? Isn't there?

Only two people in the world could have told you that. It must have been Rachel. Well, thanks a bunch. That's what I get for trusting her, it seems. Unbelievable.

I think I've had enough of this. It's all getting just a bit too fucking personal. I mean, where d'you draw the line? Are you going to want to know about when we actually did it? All the details? I bet that's all you really want to know about, isn't it? You're just ploughing through everything else, like *Fuck this shit, when do I get some hot teenage sex?* Well, I'm sorry, I'm not playing any more. It was years ago, and it wasn't even that important anyway, and I'm not into that kind of thing. I'm married now, and Chrissy wouldn't like it.

Why don't you just go and ask Damien? He'll tell you everything you want to know, in glorious technicolour detail. He'll be delighted to. I don't know why you've even been bothering with the rest of us. Oh, and it seems like Rachel's only too happy to assist him. No change there.

I've got work to do. And dogs to walk. And a wife to take care of. Did I mention we're expecting our first baby? I did, but you probably don't remember. Not that important is it, in comparison?

Day

On Friday night, I didn't sleep. My mother had a bad night. I stayed up with her until she calmed down, plugged her into the TV and then looked at the time on the video player. It was 4.57. I remember that clearly. The exact shape of those dim green digital bars on the display. Not much point, I concluded, in going to bed, and I wasn't really tired anyway. So I switched off the lights, sat on the window sill and opened the window, as I was often wont to do when feeling insomniac and somewhat poetic, it being infinitely more pleasant than sprawling on the beer-soaked carpet amidst cigarette butts and crumbs of pork scratchings.

I have a very visual memory. I have forgotten some things about the day of our enterprise, but I do remember exactly how the street looked out of the window at 4.57 that morning. It's hard to describe, but it was all about the lighting. It was the luminous, doomed dark of dawn. The kind of dark that's precious because it is ethereal. Because it must inevitably surrender to grim light and shoelaces and toothpaste and bleary-eyed commutes. I had the window open, and the air was... not exactly warm, but sort of generous. I could feel the incipient heat if I moved my fingers quickly through it.

I think I felt something coming that morning as I looked out of the window, something bigger than just the fact I was going to pop my rocks in less than twenty-four hours. Perhaps it just helps me now to think that. I didn't frame it in my head in so many words, but yes, it was there, it all seemed portentous.

85

The birds were doing their warm-up arpeggios in the trees and there seemed something mournful about that whirring and chattering. Like a dirge. And as I watched the darkness drain from the air, the amber streetlights switched off. I could see three of them from my window seat, and they clicked off one by one, not all at once. In the dark, without their heads of light, they looked like gallows. It seemed that with them something safe and friendly was extinguished, *one two three*, not just outside my window but in my chest, and I shivered suddenly. A line from Shakespeare came into my head – I was all about the Shakespeare, in those days – but I can't remember which one now.

I looked from the view outside to the view inside. Mum a mound on the sofa, finally quiet in the flickering lights from the TV. A motionless shape in the dark. I thought, *Life*, and I felt suddenly as if I wanted to cry.

I *never* cry. Not really. I wish I could.

Rachel

We'd met up on the Friday afternoon, for the last time, and agreed that we'd meet at the hotel on Saturday evening. We were very aware of the possibility of getting caught, so we had a big elaborate plan all worked out. The boys were going to get to the hotel at about six o'clock, to check in. And then Lizzie and I were going to meet them around the back of the hotel at about seven o'clock, and they'd smuggle us in by unlocking the back door and setting off the fire alarm. Nick had got hold of his dad's A–Z and found the road where the back entrance was. He'd circled the place to wait in red biro, and given it to me with the page carefully folded down. I loved him for that. I'm sure I could have found it by myself, though.

We, Lizzie and I, had told our parents we were going to sleep over at a girl from school's house, I can't remember her name. We didn't think it was safe to do the classic telling-parents-we-

were-staying-at-each-others'-houses thing. I especially didn't, seeing as my dad and Lizzie's mum were apparently quite cosy these days. Though Lizzie didn't know that, and I didn't tell her, for some reason. Don't know why not. I was ashamed. I suppose I just wanted to push it out of my mind.

We actually chose that Saturday because Lizzie's mum was away that night somewhere or other, so she only had to tell her dad what she was doing, and she could always wrap him around her little finger. We had a plan of what to tell my dad, too. We had asked this girl, this friend of mine from school, if we could drop round to pick something up. Can't remember what. Books or something, probably. Then Dad was going to drive us there and drop us off and probably actually see us go into her house, so he wouldn't suspect something was up. Then if Lizzie's mum asked him, he'd be able to vouch for us and Lizzie wouldn't get in trouble. We'd leave this girl's house after half an hour, and head for the B&B.

D'you remember life without mobile phones? They changed everything, didn't they? I sometimes think that maybe things wouldn't have gone wrong at all, if we'd had mobile phones back then. If we'd been able to talk to each other a little more easily, a little quicker, with a little more privacy. If we'd been able to warn each other – that someone else was coming, that we ourselves were coming, that he knew this or I knew that. And things would definitely have been easier to organise.

But I also sometimes think that life was more interesting without them. Remember when you had to arrange to meet someone and wait for them to turn up? And if they didn't turn up, what went through your mind? That rich, frightful series of possibilities? And you had no way of checking with them. And they had no way of saying *Sorry, bad traffic* or *Be there in 15*. Phones have probably meant fewer accidents, misunderstandings, mistakes, disappointments. Less drama. Less tragedy. Yet I sometimes wonder if this is actually a good thing. With mobile phones, there could have been no *Romeo and Juliet*, no *Tess of the D'Urbervilles*, no *Madame Bovary*.

Of course, someone dies horribly at the end of all those stories, don't they?

Anyway, the point was that we didn't speak to each other on the Saturday. It was a day of silence, and it had all already been arranged via a series of *We'll see you here, at this times*. Lizzie came over to my house in the late afternoon. Dad let her in, and she came and found me in my room. I had packed an overnight bag, as per my story. I had my pyjamas and a pair of clean underwear, and my toothbrush and hairbrush and squirty Clearasil in a flannel wash bag. And then I'd hidden some things in the side pocket of the bag. A load of the condoms that they'd given us at the clinic – not that I was terribly optimistic, or even aware of the cultural nudge-wink thing of why that would imply optimism, but just because I didn't know how difficult it might be to put them on and thought we might need to practice loads. And, a little bottle of brandy. I had found it at the back of the cupboard one day about a week beforehand, among jars of out of date curry paste and deflated quarter-bags of flour from Dad's occasional culinary endeavours. The bottle was sort of flat and hip-flask shaped. Spirits seemed more to-the-point than wine. I decided to take it with me.

Lizzie sat on the bed while I checked my last few things. It was an incredibly humid day. The early morning had been clear, but now it was one of those days when the sky was such a pale hot blue that it seemed almost white. And by midday you noticed that it actually *was* white, that somehow clouds had faded in from nowhere through the pores of the sky, and the sun was nothing more than a smear of brightness. And then the clouds ripened all afternoon, till eventually they were dark grey like smoke, and the heat was so thick that it seemed to almost have a sound. I had my bedroom light on by that time. I checked my bag through for the thousandth time. It was definitely going to rain.

D'you want some make-up then? Lizzie said. She was sitting on my bed with her back against the wall.

I had never really considered make-up before. I was vaguely aware that girls my age wore it, but I hadn't thought of wearing it myself. Kids grew up less quickly in France, and then, living with Dad... make-up was something I associated with Mum when she used to go out to dinner with Dad, and with women in films. Dark red mouths, and thick powder that smelled of perfume, and eyeshadow in exotic shades. I didn't associate make-up with *me*.

D'you wear it? I said to Lizzie.

Of course. Can't you tell? She looked amused.

I peered at her face, got as close as I dared. *No, I... I don't think I can,* I said. *What are you wearing?*

Foundation. Concealer. She pointed to her chin, where the faintest shadow of a blemish sat. *Blusher. Mascara. And just some Vaseline on my lips.* Her lips always looked like she'd just licked them. That was Vaseline then. I wondered vaguely if Vaseline didn't have something to do with petrol. I thought I'd heard it used somewhere like that.

Wow, I said, because I felt like some response was expected of me. *Well... I don't know. It's not very me. Maybe another time.*

You'll have to learn to wear it at some point, won't you? she said. She looked puzzled and a bit hurt.

I suppose so, I said.

Well, why not now? You're — we're about to do it, she said, and she smiled a huge big beaming smile that split up the beauty of her face. Now, that was a funny thing about Lizzie. She was so beautiful, except when she smiled. It feels kind of terrible to say that, because people are supposed to be more beautiful when they smile, not less, aren't they? But the opposite was true of her. I always thought it was just me, but then once I said it to Day, years later, and he said he'd always thought that too.

Okay then, I said, *but you'll have to do it for me.*

So I sat on my bed and closed my eyes. Lizzie got out her make-up bag and poked at my face with brushes and pencils and smoothed it with sponges. Strange new textures and smells and feelings, all of it. The foundation felt greasy and smelled like raw potatoes – but I don't know why I thought that, since raw potatoes don't really smell, do they? The Vaseline actually didn't taste or smell like much at all. At the end my face felt wet and brittle at the same time. Lizzie stood back and looked at me deliberately, then took out some powder and blotted first her own nose and forehead, then mine.

It's so hot, she said. *We're going to sweat loads.*

I looked in the mirror. It looked bizarre. It *felt* bizarre.

Oh, don't get me wrong, it was definitely not one of those moments where the ugly duckling (i.e. the stunning petite actress previously cleverly disguised as a munter by a pair of *thick framed glasses*) looks in the mirror after being made over and suddenly realises she's a beautiful swan and she's going to get the prom king after all. This is no fairy tale. Certainly not a Hollywood film. I mean, you watch those films to feel like things are simple, don't you? You know who to like, and who to trust, and who's a bad apple, and who's there for comic relief, and who will come through in the end. And you have to like *someone.* That's important, isn't it? It'd be a terrible Hollywood film that was just full of slightly unpleasant people talking about not much at all. Which is kind of how I feel like we must all be coming across to you now. Ugh – you probably like Father Creevey best, don't you? He's doing his twinkly-eyed old cynic schtick, I bet. Well, just remember, I warned you about him. That's all I'll say.

Anyway, make-up. Not like in the films. I was still kind of chubby and had weird hair and a normal-looking face. But I did look somehow different. I looked, I felt – I don't know. Smooth. Impregnable. Prepared. Put it this way: I understood why warriors of all sorts of times and races used to wear war paint to go into battle.

Lizzie put her hand on my far shoulder as we stood looking in the mirror. Like a proud parent, I thought. It was the first time she'd touched me voluntarily, I think. We weren't one of those linking, clutching, three-legged pairs of girlfriends. She didn't invite physical contact. Except from Day, of course. She said, *Yeah. Nice.*

So, then we were ready, and we went downstairs and Dad got the car keys and drove us to this other friend's house, which was at the far end of Sale, on that long road just before you hit the roundabout on your way to Altrincham. Just five minutes' walk from the hotel.

Dad looked at me oddly in the car. We both sat in the back seat, Lizzie and I, and I could see Dad peering at me in the rear-view mirror as he drove. I wondered if he knew, or suspected, what was going to happen, what we'd planned. But then I realised he probably just noticed I was wearing make-up.

Michel

I had known for a while, of course, that it would have to stop sooner or later. Because there are different kinds of affairs. An affair is one thing, perhaps, if you meet a person and know you want to spend the rest of your life with them. In a situation like that, you can weather initial complications with the comfort of thinking how you might look back and laugh at it together ruefully in years to come, while your children play around you on the floor, or something. But this? No. This was not like that. The whole time it was going on, I would imagine my future, and she wasn't around. It was a selfish affair, on my part.

I know I sound like a bad person. I probably am a bad person. But you argue yourself into something like that. You ask yourself, *Don't I deserve this? The world has screwed me. If it means a little happiness after all this, why shouldn't I screw the world* back? *My wife died. I'm lonely. My daughter is growing distant from me. I'm tired. I'm stressed about my work...* oh, there is no end to the reasons you can give yourself why it's okay for you to sleep with your neighbour's wife. *She knows what she's getting herself into*: that was another one, a particularly bad one. Oh, and let's not forget *I've been honest with her.* That's perhaps the most craven excuse of all.

I'll tell you something about honesty. There is no such thing. Honesty cannot exist where the scales are out of balance between two people, like they were in this case. You can say to a woman, *Things are complicated, I'm confused.* What do you think she hears? I'll tell you. She hears, *I just need to get over my confusion and then I will love you. Have patience.* Or you can say to her, *I can't be with you. I'm sorry. You deserve a better man,* and she will hear, *I want to be a better man. Help me become one.* You can say to her, *Look! I don't want to be with you,* and she hears, *You have changed everything. You have made me question my deepest convictions. I am terrified and this is self-defence on my part, a flimsy shield for my poor wounded heart. Just persist. I need you to help me.*

I'm not exaggerating here. I sound like a misogynist perhaps, but I mean this as an observation – a bewildered observation – and not as a complaint or criticism. Honesty cannot exist between two such people. There must be mutual love or silence, those are the only two ways. I tried to tell Rachel this once, when I had had a little too much to drink and memories of affairs with women were restless in my mind. Eventually I found the words. I said, *Rachel – if a boy likes you, he will act as if he likes you.* As I recall, she looked at me from under her fringe and said, *Er, yeah?*

Now I feel guilty. I mean, I always feel guilty about the memory of the affair itself, but now I'm worried I'm not representing it to you with accuracy, that my own distaste at myself has rubbed off on *her* in your mind. That I'm guilty of doing just what I accused *her* of earlier. It's not that there was nothing good about her. No, that was far from the case. She has a loving heart. Too loving, perhaps. She makes people hate her by loving them too hard. Yes, no matter how difficult she is, one cannot look at Kathleen and see the desperation of her love, and know a little of her history, and not conclude that, all in all, she has been more sinned against than sinning. Maybe it was that which drew me to her first – aside from her beauty, I mean. Her hunger to love. *For* love.

Although, it is true that this hunger didn't seem to extend to Paul much. Paul is her husband – though I heard that they are now divorced, but he was her husband at the time. You know him, yes? He's alright. A decent man, you would call him. He is quiet, he works hard, he doesn't look for trouble. The two of them, Kathleen and Paul, got married under difficult circumstances, which has always been part of Kathleen's… well, the problems she has, they date back to then, I think. The two of them were probably never right for each other. She told me several times that she never really loved him, but that he seemed to offer her something precious at the time. *He seemed like a rock, and turned out to be a millstone,* I think she once said. Or maybe it was me who said that. She has always been torn between despising him on the one hand, and on the other frantically trying to compensate for a feeling that she was somehow tarnished by her history. Scared, of both her own capacity to hurt him and of his… disapproval, I suppose? Letting him down. And when she's scared, she lashes out. That is just her way.

This is all my reading of her story, though, so don't take it as gospel truth.

I didn't really think that there was much love there, so it didn't bother me as much as it would if they were an otherwise happy couple. I felt worse about the children. I felt worst about Rachel.

It was the fact that I knew Rachel *knew*, after the time when she and Kathleen caught each other in our house, which made me realise I had to end the whole thing. I could not carry on being ashamed in front of my daughter. I remember thinking, *Even the loneliness isn't as bad as this.*

So I asked Kathleen to meet me on the Saturday evening, yes, *that* Saturday evening, to talk. We had booked a hotel room. The Best Western, in Salford Quays. That was where we always met when she, when *we* wanted to spend the night together.

On the Friday evening, I tried to talk to Rachel, who was looking up at me every now and then with her mother's eyes. I couldn't bring myself to tell her straight, so I kept telling her things about failure and compassion instead, big vague billowing words that could have been taken to mean anything or nothing. I could tell she wasn't listening.

Anyway, on the Saturday, I drove Rachel and Lizzie out to their friend's house. Rachel looked different. She was wearing make-up. That was a clue about what they were up to. I wondered if I should say anything, as I drove them there. I had an impulse for a short moment to play the stern father, to give a word of coded or uncoded warning. But then I thought about what I would be doing later on that night. So I put my eyes back on the road, and I kept on driving.

Karen Cox

So, these boys came by, like the person on the phone had said they would. The bigger one, the good-looking one, was all like, *Oh, our dad called a few days ago to reserve a room, it's about the renovation.* He seemed like a nice lad, very polite. I didn't really remember the call, but the reservation was in the book alright, so I gave them the key and told them what time breakfast was at. The smaller one asked how it was possible to have your eggs done. Seemed very concerned that he couldn't have them done some fancy way, I remember. I said, *Sorry, it's boiled, fried or scrambled, take your pick.*

By the way – the police said that he made the call in the first place. To make the reservation, you know. Don't know how me or Steve or whoever took the call could have thought he was his dad, if that was the truth. He might have talked all posh, but he *sounded* young. I don't mean he had a squeaky voice or anything, just that… he *sounded* young. You know, cocky.

Anyway, the other one, the polite one, seemed a bit embarrassed. I thought he was probably the older brother.

No. Sorry. I'm getting mixed up. All this, the eggs stuff, was when they came to pay the money, which was actually a few days in advance. At least, I think that's the way it happened. Then when they came that day, on the Saturday, the day it happened, it was just a case of giving them the room key.

Oh, like I've said before, I can't really remember. This was so long ago, what, fifteen years now? I couldn't even remember that well when the police came round. Just bear in mind that, you know, I had other customers too. We had eight rooms, and it was the summer so at least five of 'em would've been full. I really didn't give these kids a second thought. And I don't think that says anything about me, either. Just that I was a busy woman trying to make a living.

Anyway, I gave them the room key. I gave it to the older looking one, the nice polite one. Not the eggs one. I put them in room seven, on the second floor.

Yeah, it was a twin room. That's a bit dodgy in itself, isn't it? Four of them in a twin room, we found out later on. I mean, boys will be boys, but I don't know how they persuaded the girls to go for that. I wouldn't have agreed to that back when I was that age, I can tell you. Not that I would now either! You know what I mean. Kids these days, though. Or those days. Whatever. They're something else.

Day

Now, I know what you're going to say. One room? Two couples? You're going to wrinkle your nose up, aren't you? *This is not how it's supposed to be!* you're going to protest with a trembling tear of disillusionment in your eye – if you should be the romantic type, that is, with a rosy vision of the tender First Time. Or perhaps, should you happen to be more of the sanctimonious breed, the sexual conservative, a lights-off, missionary-only, pyjamas–on–as–far–as–physically-possible prude, then you'll be scandalised. Perhaps this might even give you pause about our characters. Shed new light on what followed later. *Well, I should have seen it coming,* you'll mutter inwardly. *Group sex! Saucy romp! Orgy! At that age! I ask you.*

Empathise a little! Remember my initial rant, when we first met, about the constraints upon one when one is but a puny, powerless stripling of fourteen years? We found it hard enough to find a hotel room for sixty quid, even in such a dive as the Brooklands Best Bed and Breakfast. What chance did we have of finding two, for that paltry sum? (No offence, Nick. Pater Stu's reward system should have been more generous really, considering all the diligent labour I put into your English assignments.) And, well, it wasn't like that. We were going to be drunk, after all. And I had got hold of some of the friendlier narcotics from an associate of mine. And it was going to be dark. Not dark enough in the end, but we'll come to that. Oh, and we had music! Nick had brought his charming petite compact disc player, complete with miniature speakers, which he solemnly produced from his rucksack when we finally got into the room. Want to know what he had on there? Classical music. It was adorable.

But I get ahead of myself. The point I'm trying to make is that it may have been the same room but it certainly wasn't anything approaching this, this Roman excess, this salacious tabloid Holy Grail, this *orgy*.

But, at the same time, believe it or not, the closeness actually felt oddly appropriate. It was always the four of us, like I've told you. We had grown up together. We had planned it all together. We had nearly got caught together. We had regrouped together. And now we were here. This, this tender togetherness, was something that was not only tolerable but also oddly appropriate. It would have been weird, not to mention sad, to be alone, you know. Well, not *alone*. Separated. Compartmentalised. You know what I mean.

Does that sound strange? Why should it? Isn't it accepted that when you go through most rites of passage you have friends or family behind you? With you, holding your hand all the way? Well, why not with this one? I'm afraid that maybe we've indulged our sense of taboo too far, as a society, in this respect. We've let the censors and the Bowdlerisers infiltrate our consciousnesses too far. It's a big step to take by yourself, after all, sex. It's so easy for it to go wrong.

Funny, by the way, is it not, that I still defend this sexual sociability? When ironically it was the very fact that we were all in the same room that, like so many other factors, led to my arrest? If we'd been more prudish, or a little richer, I could have got away with anything I liked.

We're getting there now. Your patience is close to being rewarded. Not long to go. *Courage, mon brave.* You have been a most satisfactory auditor.

Lizzie

There was a back door to the hotel, through the kitchen, that led out to the bins and that. The boys had found it when they went there the first time, to pay. We waited there, me and Rachel, for ages. We ran out of conversation. That happened quite a lot. I always felt a bit stupid around Rachel, even stupider than usual. I still do. Do you find that? Or is it just me?

He was late. But he came eventually, and got us. He came

from the street, he'd gone out of the front door and come round the block to where we were waiting. We all crouched by the wall and waited for the fire alarm, 'cause that was the signal. Nick was going to set off the fire alarm, and we'd sneak in through the back entrance while everyone went out into the street.

But then something went wrong. Nick turned up. Coming from the street, the same as Day. Day looked at him and was like, *What the fuck are you doing, you're supposed to be setting off the alarm!* Nick was just like, *I tried! It's fucking broken. I smashed the glass and nothing happened.* Day started laughing and laughing, kind of silently, and just saying, *Typical, typical, typical.* Rachel was like, *Well what do we do now then?* And Nick said, *There's nobody on reception right now. Let's just walk in.* Day was laughing and laughing, so hard he was nearly choking, and now he was saying, *Genius, genius.* Nick was all grinning and said, *Come on then, quick or she'll be back.* So we walked round the front, and went through the door and up the stairs and into the room like normal people. It was easy.

Day

Alas! – the Brooklands Best Bed and Breakfast has gone the way of all worldly things and is no more. I believe the initial burst of publicity and consequent prurient custom after the story got out was not enough to stop it being closed by local authority food law enforcement officers in 1999. Rather Al Capone and his tax returns, no? It was bulldozed sometime near the turn of the millennium. I went back to look at the building site. There is now a funeral director's where the scene of my crime used to be.

Rachel

We all felt exultant, I think. We were in, we were safe. Nobody could stop us now. I remember Day flipping the lock into place and saying, *Welcome, ladies, to the scene of the crime,* and he looked at me and smiled, and I smiled back at him.

As if to give us a kind of approval, the weather broke right then and it started raining. A waft of cool air blew the net curtain aside and the window sill was spattered with rain drops. I walked over, and pulled the net curtain aside and closed the window, and put the lock into place there too. I could see, in the reflection in the window in front of me, Nick starting to pull out the booze we had brought from our bags. Lizzie sat on one of the beds and drew her legs up and started rolling a spliff. I saw the shape of Day wander over to me.

He stood next to me by the window. *You look different,* he said.

I've got Lizzie's make-up on, I said, and touched my own face. *She made me over.*

We were looking at each other in the glass of the window. Not turning to face each other. Having a conversation with each others' reflections, sort of, against the backdrop of the murky rain outside. Looking at him via the glass made me bold. *D'you like it?* I said. *Do I look different?*

And then a funny thing happened. I saw his face in the glass pucker into a strange expression. It was almost like he rolled his eyes. Then he looked confused. Then he sort of half put out a hand to my face, then drew it back and ruffled up his own hair instead.

You look better without, he said, eventually. And then he turned and looked at me properly, at my real face. I saw him do it while I still watched the reflections. He did it for a long time.

Eventually I turned so we stood face to face. *Well, I'll take it off then,* I said.

Just a few brief, innocuous words. Nothing to speak of. The other two must have heard, and they didn't even look up from their silly loud conversation, didn't even notice. But it changed everything.

I watched him walk over to take the rolled spliff from Lizzie, and he didn't say thanks. He took it and sat on the bed and lit it in between his cupped hands, and then he looked at me again, across the room. He looked puzzled.

I turned back to the window. It was raining harder than ever, the rain sounded like handfuls of gravel being chucked against the glass. I pulled the net curtain across, then drew the curtains. They were horrible, limp, mustard-coloured things. Dirty. I went into the little bathroom to wash my hands. I washed my face too, with three or four big lovely sluices of water; took all the make-up off that Lizzie had spent so long applying with her painstaking jabs and smudges. I looked at myself in the mirror and wiped the orange and black and brown streaks away with wet toilet paper.

Everything had changed.

But I don't mean that I didn't want to do the plan anymore. I knew it meant more to him than that. It meant more to me too.

So, we did it. Just as we'd planned.

It panned out pretty much as you might expect. We all drank a bit of brandy and a bit of whisky and a bit of vodka, and we smoked a load of cigarettes and a couple of spliffs – we knew that the fire alarm didn't work, at least, so we didn't have to worry about that. I felt high, and I just kept feeling higher. I was thinking about Day, free Day, future Day, but also, this might sound weird, about Nick. I looked at him, he was holding my hand and stroking my leg… and I don't know if it was the weed or the booze or love, a kind of understudy love, but even though I knew from that moment that it was over, I felt so fond of him. I thought, *I want to give him this. He's put in his hours.*

Those were the exact words in my head. *He's put in his hours.* Is that… shocking? Callous? I've told some people since then that I thought of it like that, and they're often shocked. Or pretend to be. But I'm not sure that I see why. Don't you think it was easier to be callous when you were young? It's almost like your heart starts out like the rest of your body, strong and firm and healthy, and as you get older it softens and sags and defaults on you. Can't take as much. Lets you down when you least expect it. If you're unlucky, the cancers creep in. Well, that's what I think.

Anyway. Everyone seemed high at this point, you know, not just me. It was infectious. I looked around at all their faces, and it was one of those moments in life where you can feel the tectonic plates shifting. The end of one era and the beginning of another. And after a bit, we started kissing, in our couples, in between breaths of cigarette and swigs from the bottle. We moved to lie on the beds where it would take place. Nick and I were on the left-hand bed nearest to the window. Left-hand if you were standing at the foot of the bed, I mean. Day and Lizzie were on the right-hand one. It was dark with rain, and we left the lights off.

Nick put on this music, on this little music player he'd brought along. It was something like his mum's *100 Greatest Classical Hits*. Something like that. So weird. But kind of funny. I guess he didn't know about Marvin Gaye yet. Neither did I, to be fair.

I don't know which songs, exactly. All familiar ones. From adverts, I suppose, and the soundtracks to period dramas.

He lay on top of me under the covers. But it was me who made the moves. I took off my top, and took off his T-shirt — I got it stuck on his head, so I giggled a bit about that. He sort of laughed too, but then he kissed me hard as if he was trying to stop my mouth, stop me laughing. I unzipped his fly and pulled his trousers down — more trouble around the socks — and then I started touching him in the way you're supposed to. *How do you know what to do?* he whispered in my ear, and I just giggled again because I didn't know how, it was as if I had always known. Original sin, I suppose.

Then the underwear. The weird first-time feel of someone else's skin on mine, there. We didn't bother with the preliminaries for long, though. I just wanted to get it done. I took him in one hand and the condom in the other — I'd unwrapped it beforehand, on purpose — and unrolled it onto him carefully, and then said, *Just do it. Just do it*. He started to work it in. It hurt. Not excruciating pain, just a kind of very sharp pinching. But I just concentrated on breathing and when he said, *Are you alright?* I said, *Yeah, yeah, don't worry, I think it's supposed to hurt.*

That first working it in was the painful part. Then it started to be… nice.

I don't mean that I came, or anything. Nobody comes on their first time. No girls, I mean. Certainly not when they're fourteen. I think it might be physically impossible. But… I don't know how I can put it. It felt good to have it there. And I liked how shell-shocked he was. Oh, I liked that. His eyes were just blanked out, and his forehead sort of bewildered. It made me feel powerful.

I was drunk and drowsy and stoned. I thought, *Nick.* I thought, *Day.* At some point the moving and the breathing of me and Nick faded out, and I heard noises from the other bed, and before I could stop myself I turned my head and I saw the two of them moving. And at that moment Day turned his head too, turned it towards me, and our eyes met. And I felt, suddenly, powerfully, real attraction, like a mighty hand opening inside me with the fingers flexing outward, and I made a noise.

Then Nick… lost it.

I don't know why I'm telling you this, but I've started so I might as well carry on. He lost it, so we didn't end up… finishing. I could tell he was upset, he kept trying to put it back in and his hand was trembling and I was whispering, *It's okay, It's okay.* And he was like, *I'm fine! I just need a minute.* And then we were in that zone of weary clichés I now know so well, and it was never going to get back on track.

We heard Day come after a minute or two. Lizzie had been making this little moaning sound for ages, and it just generally died away. Then the room was silent, except for the thudding of the rain on the window.

Day

You remember that English teacher I told you about? He had a mantra that he'd bellow at us as a supposed aid for our trite creative writing assignments. It was *Show, Don't Tell.* This little mantra has, they tell me, during the last few decades been all the rage at the various costly creative writing courses that have sprung up in our illustrious nation. The idea being, I believe, that it is somehow more noble, somehow more *generous* on the author's part, to allow the reader imaginative space and freedom to construct their own story from a bare framework of factual, sparsely reported events. The author, current vogue in the literary world dictates, should never presume to *tell* the reader anything. It's up to the reader, the mighty reader with their Waterstones-friendly buck, to decide what they think happened. The author *a la mode* is merely there to, I don't know, get them thinking, I suppose.

Damien and Lizzie lie in the right-hand bed, with the covers over them, even though it's so hot that their bodies are wet with sweat from top to toe. They're both drunk. The bottles are by the bed. Her clothes lie in puddles on the carpet next to the bottles. Only her bra and knickers remain in place. He's naked. They kiss, permanently. They touch, sporadically. He's sexually excited. She says his name, again and again, between kisses. He doesn't say hers back. He doesn't know why.

He wants to be in her. He kneels up under the covers and looks at her. He takes in what she looks like in the gloom. Pale shapes. He thinks, *Life.*

He takes her knickers off. He puts it in, bit by bit, slowly. She makes noises. He says, *Are you okay?* She doesn't reply. So he puts it in further, in one big push. He moves forward, and back. Again and again. Sometimes he looks straight down at her – her eyelashes wet, her mouth open, the way strands of her hair are stuck with sweat to her temple. Sometimes he moves his head so her face is in his chest, and then he looks straight ahead at the headboard, which is padded and stained. He can see the swirls of coffee or the bodily fluids of others, even in the darkness. Sometimes he looks to the side. Yes, sometimes he looks to the side. He moves the whole time. He can feel the burning of the spirits on his breath, and smell them on hers. A drop of sweat drips from his cheek on to hers.

The music plays from the floor in between the two couples. Bach's Orchestral Suite No. 3 in D Major, to be precise.

It doesn't take long. He moves faster. Her noises are faster too. He doesn't hear what she says – it's one sound, again and again. Then he realises that the word she is saying, quietly, so quietly, is *no*, and the world explodes for him from inside.

Nick

I heard her say *no*. I'm pretty sure I heard her say *no*.

Rachel

I didn't hear a thing. I don't think Day did, either. He wouldn't have carried on, if he had.

I'm not saying Lizzie's lying. But… she probably just lost her nerve and wanted to stop and didn't know how to say it so she said something really quietly and he was caught up in the moment and didn't hear. Crossed wires, like I told you in the beginning. It happens. It's nobody's fault.

Nick said what he thought he remembered.

Two minutes in that scrubby little hotel room. When I think about it, it makes my head spin.

Anyway. After it finished, we all lay there for a bit. I have no idea what went through the others' heads but I felt drowsy and kind of pleased with myself and I marvelled at our own grown-upness. It didn't matter to me that we, that Nick, that we didn't finish. It was okay. We'd done it. I stroked his hair. He had his head on my chest and lay very still and I wondered if he was asleep. After a while, Day got up and walked across the room naked. He picked up some bottles, shook them. There was still some liquid sloshing in one. He brought it back to the bed. When I looked over, I saw he had Lizzie cradled in one arm and was sitting pulling on the bottle with the other. He looked over at me. *Alright, Rach,* he said.

Hi, I said.

He leaned over, careful not to disturb Lizzie, and offered me the vodka. I took it and drank.

He looked at me and mouthed, *I love you.*

We lay there and drank and listened to the rain, with two bodies in between us.

If we'd just stayed there, fallen asleep, stayed until morning and then sneaked out, things might have been different. We'd have had more time. More time to clean up and get our stuff together. But we started drinking again, and then when Lizzie and Nick woke up they started drinking with us, and pretty soon we were all on a second wind.

Everyone seemed fine. I can't highlight this enough.

As I've said before, I don't judge. I'm not saying anyone's lying. But everyone seemed fine.

So we drank some more, and then we smoked some more, and then somehow it was five o'clock in the morning. The rain had stopped and the sky was starting to get a dull kind of light in it outside the window. Day suddenly got one of his fits of hyperactivity on, and was obsessed with the idea of going for a walk. The rest of us weren't so keen I don't think. Nick definitely wasn't so keen, said something along the lines of, *Well as long as we've paid for the room we might as well use it properly,* and Day said, *Were you seriously thinking of going down for breakfast, the four of us all bright and post-coital?* and Nick said, *Be a shame not to get your fucking eggs wouldn't it?*   I didn't really get what that was about – and I could tell that it was about to get nasty and I started to think, *All they do is fight these days.* Nick said, *C'mon Rach, come back to bed, let's get a bit of sleep,* and Day said,

Bliss was it in that dawn to be alive, But to be young was very heaven.
And I looked at them both and said, *Come on, Nick, it'll be fun,*
and started putting my shoes on.

And then Day said, *Come on! Let's go! Let's go!* And started
hopping around. And we all grabbed our stuff and headed for
the door — Nick said, *Wait, aren't we going to clear this stuff up?*
And Day said, *Oh fuck that* or something along those lines, and
so we left. And as we got nearly to the bottom of the stairs,
Day grabbed my hand and said *Run,* and we started running,
ran through the reception and busted open the door and ran
out into the dawn, whooping. It was glorious.

Nick
What a fucking mess.

There were bottles of spirits, and the remains of spliffs, and
cigarettes, and condoms. Some used, some not.

Oh, and Lizzie's keys, of course, under the bed. But we didn't
know that at the time.

I said we should clear up. And Damien said, *Alright, Mum,
you go ahead. We're out of here,* and grabbed Rachel and bundled
her out of the door.

So really, what happened next was his own fault.

Lizzie
Been waiting to hear from me, have you? I bet you have.

For a long time after it happened, I thought about what
people mean when they say that word.

I'm not clever. You might have noticed. But I think I do
understand this one thing pretty well. I had to look over a load
of things. D'you want to know the important bits?

This is the actual definition of rape:

(1) It is an offence for a man to rape a woman or another man.

(2) A man commits rape if–

    (a) he has sexual intercourse with a person (whether vaginal or anal) who at the time of the intercourse does not consent to it; and

    (b) at the time he knows that the person does not consent to the intercourse or is reckless as to whether that person consents to it.

(3) A man also commits rape if he induces a married woman to have sexual intercourse with him by impersonating her husband.

Can you answer me this? If a guy and a girl are going out, and he has a twin brother, who she hates. And one day the twin brother dresses up in his brother's, the girl's boyfriend's, clothes. And he goes and finds her and lies down with her and has sex with her. Then afterwards, he tells her, *Gotcha. It's me. Tricked you.*

Was she raped?

If not, why not? She didn't agree to have sex with that exact person, did she? You could say she was forced into it. But by being deceived. That's why they have that bit in there, about pretending you're someone's husband.

Okay. Now, what about if, halfway through, she realised it was the wrong brother? And she said, *No.* She didn't say, *Stop.* I can't explain to you why she didn't think to say the precise word *Stop.* She thought *No,* so she said, *No.* He should have known what *no* meant. That's the slogan they used on the posters, isn't it? *No means no.*

Was she raped? Or was it okay for him to carry on?

Well, that's what happened to me.

Also:

> **Intercourse with a girl between thirteen and sixteen.**
> It is an offence, subject to the exceptions mentioned in this section, for a man to have unlawful sexual intercourse with a girl... under the age of sixteen.

Pretty clear, that one, isn't it? Also:

> **Administering drugs to obtain or facilitate intercourse.**
> It is an offence for a person to apply or administer to, or cause to be taken by, a woman any drug, matter or thing with intent to stupefy or overpower her so as thereby to enable any man to have unlawful sexual intercourse with her.

Also:

> **Indecent assault on a woman.**
> (1) It is an offence, subject to the exception mentioned in subsection (3) of this section, for a person to make an indecent assault on a woman.
> (2) A girl under the age of sixteen cannot in law give any consent which would prevent an act being an assault for the purposes of this section.

Guilty, I reckon. Guilty on loads of counts.

I saw. I knew. While we were doing it, while he was... while we were...

It wasn't till the next day that I was completely sure. But at that moment I knew. I said *no*. And he didn't stop. Nothing happened.

That was my first time.

108

Rachel

Has Lizzie been throwing the book at you? Yes. She does that a lot. It's like she's figured out this one precious piece of knowledge and she can't let go of it. The sad thing – one of the sad things about this situation – is that Lizzie's knowledge is totally out of date. The Sexual Offences Act came along in 2003 and now everything's different. I've tried to explain this to her. A number of times. But she doesn't get it. She says, *That was then. This is now.*

She's talking about two different things. She's talking about rape and Unlawful Sexual Intercourse, USI they call it apparently. Now, from my point of view, the only thing that could possibly make it rape is if she told him to stop – that's one thing, and I've already told you that I'm sure she didn't. So, rape's out. It's not on, in my opinion, to conflate rape, real rape, with that USI stuff. This idea that girls under sixteen *can't* consent. That they're not real people. That is – excuse my French – a crock of shit. I'm evidence to the contrary.

The legislation these days – it still says that if you do it with anyone under sixteen you can be put away for up to five years. Which is pretty stupid, I think. But, the difference is, there are guidelines now, for the prosecutors, which basically beg them to turn a blind eye. One of those funny little hiccups in English law. This is what they say:

> *'It is* not *in the public interest to prosecute children who are of the same or similar age and understanding that engage in sexual activity, where the activity is truly consensual for both parties and there are no aggravating features, such as coercion or corruption. In such cases, protection will normally be best achieved by providing education for the children and young people and providing them and their families with access to advisory and counselling services. This is the intention of Parliament.'*

While I rather resent the idea that anybody who wants to have sex under sixteen needs education and counselling, it's a damn sight better than the offensive bullshit that Lizzie can't stop quoting.

Day

Mmm. Yes. I have heard all that before, a number of times. She left one important bit out though.

> ### Intercourse with an idiot or imbecile.
> *It is an offence for a man to have unlawful sexual intercourse with a woman whom he knows to be an idiot or imbecile.*

I suggested to my solicitor, in my hour of most potent bitterness, that perhaps I should be tried under this particular section of the legislation. I don't think she was amused.

Nick

I knew when she put on her shoes. They were lace-up trainers, quite new, blue and white. Most people do their trainers up once and then just slide them on and off after that, but Rachel always undid her shoes to take them off and did the laces back up when she put them back on. She took good care of her things. I watched her fingers while she did the bows. I knew there was no point in looking at her face, because she wasn't looking at me.

But if I hadn't known at that point, then I would have realised when the four of us walked home. They walked up ahead, the two of them. It was like they had forgotten that Lizzie and I existed. It was like they had forgotten what we'd just done. Can you believe that? Straightaway! Straight afterwards! I can't... I can't get my head around it, even after so long.

Poor Lizzie didn't get it. She was trying to walk faster to

catch up with them, trying to listen in to the silly stuff they were saying to each other – lovers' talk, I understand that now – and she kept looking at me as if to say, *Come on, hurry up, let's catch them up,* or as if she was exasperated at me for being slow. I didn't have much sympathy to spare for anyone else at that point, but what I did have was for her. At one point I said, *Leave it, Lizzie, there's no point*, or something like that. Then I felt mean. She looked at me as if she was hurt. I didn't want to talk, but I had questions in my mind, about Damien and the fact I thought I had heard her say *no…* but I was so bloody confused, and I was starting to get a stinking hangover. I just wanted to go to bed. There was still a little part of me hoping that I'd wake up in the morning, the proper morning I mean, after I'd gone back to bed, and that everything would be fine. That this would all have been the great, fun, awesome thing we thought it was going to be, and not – as I was starting to suspect – a fucking terrible mistake.

Rachel

When we'd got a decent distance from the hotel we slowed down and started walking. We all walked back together, but I walked with Day and Lizzie walked with Nick. Day was right, it was a beautiful morning. We were the only souls in the world.

It was Sunday. Everything had changed and we were grown-ups now, that's how it felt. But, you know, life has a funny way of cutting you down when you feel like you're tallest. We had no way of knowing what was waiting for us at home.

Michel

We met in the hotel room that night. How many times did we meet in a hotel room, altogether, I wonder? It was, looking back on it, an affair of clichés. Clichés, by definition, are powerless when it comes to expressing love, are they not? But they are actually rather good for expressing sadness, I think. The sadness of sameness. The sadness of realising that your dreams come from a conveyor belt.

You know, when we first started meeting in hotel rooms, I used to bring her champagne. Champagne from the little wine merchant on Victoria Street. I'd bring crystal glasses to drink it from too. But as the relationship lengthened and dulled, I started bringing her regular wine instead, a bottle of red or even warm white picked up from Sainsburys, or the Co-op. Once, I got it from a petrol station. And for the first time, this time, the last time, I didn't bring her anything.

She kissed me when I arrived. She always kissed me so hard, it almost hurt. It is not actually pleasant, that. Well, maybe it is for some men. Not for me. Roberta always used to kiss so softly, little butterfly kisses around the edge of my mouth, so that I almost didn't know if I was being kissed or just breathed on. It was hypnotic. The difference between how Roberta kissed and how Kathleen kissed was like the difference between being asked something that you've been dying to tell, and being told something you need to hear, but don't want to.

Still, that doesn't mean it wasn't arousing. Desire is a strange thing.

She said, *God I've missed you, I wanted to call you, I didn't know if it was safe, I was thinking about you all today…* et cetera. The things we say to avoid listening to silence. I nodded, I opened my mouth and closed it again, I accepted her kisses.

But I didn't want to get into a situation where I slept with her and then broke it off with her while we lay together. Even I had my limits. So I just said it as soon as I could, as soon as she stopped talking. I said, *Kathleen, we need to talk.* Those tired words.

I know, she said. *I know. I'm going to leave him.*

I said, *What?*

She said, *I'm leaving him. I'm leaving Paul. I can't do this anymore.* She looked at me eagerly, waiting for my joy.

It was the worst thing she could possibly have said. I thought, *I can't do it now,* and then I thought, *No, I must, it will be worse if she leaves him and tries to come to me.* I said, to string out the time, *What about the children?*

Her face quivered. *I know,* she said. *I know. But I need you. And you need me. They'll learn to understand. They're getting older.*

I looked at the tray of condiments by the TV, the freeze-dried coffee and tea bags and little pots of long-life milk that we would not use the next morning. I said, *I wish you hadn't said that.*

Kathleen

I lay in the hotel room after he'd gone, just straight on the bed looking at the ceiling and shaking. I remember I still had my shoes on, my best red shoes. There was a little corner of my brain nagging me, saying, *Take your shoes off, Kath, come on, it's dirty to have them on the bed.*

It was punishment. I felt like it was punishment for what I'd done. I lay there all night, thinking, and by the end I could only blame myself. Of course he didn't want me. I didn't *deserve* to be wanted. What kind of a man would want someone like me, someone who would give herself away like that, who didn't respect her own husband, who didn't even respect herself? I felt the same way that night as I did back when I was fifteen.

That was when I started crying.

Love… that kind of love… it's the enemy. You've got to be careful, look out for it. That's what I was always trying to tell Lizzie. I may have been hard on her, but I just wanted to stop her making the same mistakes. Stop her turning out like me.

Lizzie

When I got back to my house that morning, I was dead upset. But it kind of kept coming in waves, switching on and off. Sometimes I'd think I imagined it, that everything was actually

fine, and I'd be thinking to myself, *Don't be jealous! It's Rachel.*
You can't be jealous of Rachel, it's stupid. And thinking about how,
after all, I was still Day's girlfriend. I knew he loved me.

And then everything would like shift in my mind, and I'd
remember very clearly that moment of looking up and seeing
his face turned to Rachel and Rachel's towards his and they
were watching each other.

And it felt, oh, I can't even tell you how it felt. I can't. I
thought, I kept thinking, *No, it's me and him. It's him and me. It's*
always been him and me. Not him and her. It didn't make any sense.

But then, the way they had walked home together, going off
together like that – I didn't get it. I'd tried to catch them up,
tried to walk quicker so all four of us were walking together,
and Nick just looked at me and was like, *Leave it, Lizzie. There's*
no point. And I thought, *Of course, he'll be upset too, about Rachel.*
And that made me really frightened.

We all got back to our houses about seven in the morning,
I think. I was still drunk, I didn't usually drink that much. I
wanted some cereal and to clean my teeth and wash my face
and go to bed, and then I'd feel better. Then I'd have a day in
bed with magazines, and I'd be fine in time for when Mum got
back and church in the evening. I got to my front door, walking
really quietly up to it, and then I got my bag out for my keys.
I spent ages groping around for them, but they weren't there.
I started to panic and I tipped everything out on the doorstep,
there was a big pile of tissues and coins and make-up and my
spare clothes I hadn't used in the end, and I was thinking like,
Where the fuck are they? Where the fuck? Where the fuck?

I'd lost them. I'd left them somewhere. I tried the handle
but it was locked. So I went round to Day's but there was no
answer when I rang the buzzer. I thought about going to Nick's
or Rachel's, but they had real parents and that, so I couldn't
just ring the doorbell and disturb them. There'd be too many
questions. My head hurt, I felt sick. So I just sat in our garden

shed and sort of dozed until later on in the morning, when people were up and about. I heard Dad putting the bins out, so I knew the door was open and I was able to go in as if I'd just arrived home that moment. I said hi to Dad and then I went straight up to bed and fell asleep. I thought I'd decide what to do when I woke up.

Michel

When I had calmed her down, I left her there in the hotel room and went home. I paid upfront for the room. I would have driven her home, of course, but she had her own car, and she couldn't get back earlier than originally scheduled or Paul would suspect. I didn't want her to ruin everything with him because she was upset. I tried to tell her that but I must have said it wrong – she started screaming at me then, she even went to hit me.

I got home. I didn't feel like sleeping, so I made myself coffee and had a shower, and then I sat up in the living room with a book. I consoled myself with thinking that this would be the start of a good phase with Paul for her. She told me how she felt rescued by him when they first got married, and how those first few years were the happiest. I told myself that maybe this would be the start of things getting better for her. That she would feel she'd stepped back from a precipice, and was glad to be safe.

Of course, it didn't work out like that in the end, because of the children.

Rachel came home by herself at about seven o'clock in the morning, so I knew something was wrong. She said she'd had a fight with her friends, but I didn't believe her. I tried to read her face. I thought she looked happy, but it was hard to tell. Mainly she looked tired.

You should have telephoned me to pick you up, I said.

It's okay, I wanted the walk, she said.

I told her she should be careful walking around at that time.

It's okay... she started saying, then changed her mind and said, *There was nobody about. I'm going back to bed, I think.*

She went upstairs. I went back into the living room and picked up my coffee. I remember it had gone cold, and one of those little wispy flies had fallen into it and drowned. It was floating on the surface. I went to the kitchen sink and poured it away, and stared out of the window at the garden. I thought about my mother. Kathleen's body. The loneliness. My daughter. I wondered how I ended up like this. Then, it can only have been a few minutes after Rachel went upstairs, the doorbell rang. It was Damien. He was in a terrible state.

Jordan

Not much to tell, is there?

Didn't think there was anything different about my mum that night. She was just like usual, I thought. I got in like about one or something and said, *Alright, Mum* and she said, *Alright* and I ate my chips and watched some telly and went to bed. Day wasn't there, guessed he was out with his bird.

Then I woke up sometime in the morning and heard a load of shouting. Came out of the bedroom and found Day shaking Mum and screaming, like. Proper screaming.

Day

It's unfortunate that you cannot now meet my mother. She would add a certain something to your line-up of bickering attestants. Let's call it colour. Oh, she wouldn't have first-hand knowledge of all these events in the same way as the four of us do – even some of the parents and peripherals appear to be thrusting in a useful penn'orth here and there don't they? – but I suppose, in a way, she knew me best. A parent, any parent, generally has useful things to say about their child. The first word I said, the nightmares I had, the childish lispings, the stick-men drawings... surely those could have exposed to you some indication of my hopes, dreams, fears, propensities, the kind of reprobate I always was or was gradually becoming. I think you'd have managed to glean something from her that you could have twisted into the shape of a clue. She's dead now. I'm sorry. Move along, nothing to see here.

Rachel once said to me that I give the impression that I despised my mother. That's not true. I understood her. If you really understand someone, you can't despise them. Doesn't mean you can't resent them all the same.

Oh, very well, since you're here anyway, and since my mother can't tell you anything about me, I shall tell you something about her. Save you a wasted trip.

My mother was an artist, and she used the medium of degradation. Not for her paint or prose or pottery. Not for her textiles and jewellery, amateur dramatics, or the medium of expressive dance. Like the great mass of unrecognised artists, she made a tragedy with the stuff of her own life. She failed, and failed, and failed, with exquisite excess. She hurled her physical and mental health, her personal safety, the welfare of her children and dependents to the winds, in pursuit of the ultimate dereliction. She *strove* for it.

Perhaps this is the respect in which most I take after her. But I'm something of a poor scion. I'm afraid – are you starting to figure this out? – that my art means little to me without an audience. I need the intoxicant of applause, or the stimulant of catcalls. Even a shocked silence is better than nothing, as long as there is somebody *there*. Do you see what I mean? Do you start to get it? My mother's art was pure. She pursued pain and misery and notoriety just for herself, heedless of effect. I can't do that. Neither could my father.

What I'm working up to, I suppose, is smack.

When I came in that morning, I didn't initially know anything was wrong. My mother was lying sprawled face down on the floor next to the sofa, but that wasn't terribly unusual, to be honest. I went to her, to shake her as usual, and can you credit it, I remember thinking cruel things about her as I did so. Nothing happened, and then I realised I could smell sick. I rolled her over; her face was covered in it. I called to her. I slapped her face. Then I called to my brother, who emerged from his room and stood there like the proverbial lemon. I picked up the phone to call 999. There was no dial tone, and I remembered that I'd meant to pay the phone bill.

Michel

It took a little while to just get him to calm down and tell us what had happened. Then of course we called the ambulance and hurried to the flat. The two boys went with the paramedics and I drove Rachel to Wythenshawe Hospital after them. I didn't feel I could leave them, really.

She had overdosed. Which meant she had stopped breathing. That's what the doctor told us, while his eyes flickered between me and the boys as if unsure which had more authority. But, he went on to say – why do they not say this at the very beginning? – they had treated her successfully with some drug, and they thought she might recover. But there was more. Some vomit had gone into her airway, and there might be brain damage. They wanted to keep her in the medical assessment unit for observation.

There was another doctor, a children's doctor I think, who wanted to see the boys. They asked them some questions about family and friends. And, as I waited with Rachel while all this happened – we waited for hours, or so it seemed – it became obvious to me that despite the fact I hardly knew them, I would have to take them home. Take care of them for a while. They asked me some questions, and took my details, and went away to make some calls – probably to check I wasn't a paedophile.

We got back to the house early on Sunday evening. I thought the best thing I could do was feed them.

I was horrified. At the flat, I mean. At the mother. At everything. I never knew things were like this for Damien. I had only met him a few times, I admit, but still. One generally looks at one's teenage daughters' friends with a critical eye, doesn't one? But when I had met him, he had always seemed very... I suppose I want to say impressive in some ways. Not rough at all. His younger brother looked more like that type. Rude and sullen, what Rachel called 'scally'. But Damien... I suppose what I'm trying to say, and I don't know why it's so hard given how things turned out in the end, is that I liked him. I still do. It's a good thing too, really.

Lizzie

I woke up later on that day, on the Sunday, after I'd had a sleep, and I felt a bit better. The keys were still a problem, though. I thought, *I could just say I left them on the bus or something*. But there was something niggling at the back of my mind, there was something I hadn't thought of. I felt a bit panicky, and I remember I thought, *I'll have to ask Day what to do*. He always knew what to do.

And then I was glad, at the thought I had a reason to go back and see him. So I went round. I rang the buzzer, but there was still nobody there. I started to get worried. I stood on the street and looked around for a bit, and wondered where else he'd be. Either Nick's or Rachel's.

I can't tell you why I went round to Rachel's first. I can't tell you why I didn't ring the doorbell like I normally would. Why I stood there on the drive looking at the doorbell and listening instead. Why eventually I went through the gate at the side of the house, into the back garden. I remember watching my feet as I walked around to the kitchen window. The path was weedy and covered in slugs, you know, like it sometimes is after lots of rain. I was being careful not to tread on any, watching my trainers, so I was actually right in front of the window by the time I looked up.

They were sitting at the kitchen table just a few feet away from me, behind the glass. Neither of them had seen me.

They were sitting there and they were holding hands. Both hands in both hands, like this, stretched across the table. They were talking.

It sounds weird, I know, but I stood there for about five minutes, looking straight at them through the window. There were bushes in front of me, but if they'd just turned they would have clearly seen my head above them. But they didn't turn. They were too wrapped up in each other, too deep in conversation. I felt like a ghost. I wanted to smash my fist through the window, tear the bushes apart, throw them both against the wall, show that I was *there*.

In the end, I just walked away. They never saw me come, they never saw me go.

I went back to my house. I went into the shed, *that* shed. I put my face in my dad's gardening gloves. I couldn't cry. It was too bad for that.

Because I had given myself away like a packet of Bacardi Breezers.

Because he raped me.

Because I still loved him.

Because my mum was right.

Because I'd lost my keys. I haven't really told you about my keys yet, or – which is what I realised at that moment, in the shed, sinking my teeth into Dad's gardening gloves to stop myself from screaming – why it was so bad that I lost them. They had a key ring on them. Dad had put it on for me ages ago, because he always worried about me losing them. It was a little plastic pink key ring in the shape of a horse's head and it said *Lizzie* on the back. And then on the front there was a clear plastic bit and you could put a photo behind it. But Dad had put a piece of paper in instead, with my name and phone number written on it.

Rachel

I know there were more important things going on. I know this probably makes me a bad person. But I kept thinking, *He came to me, he came to me.*

That afternoon, we came back from the hospital and Jordan went off somewhere, and Dad went to do some work, and Day and me sat at the kitchen table and drank tea. We talked about everything. I can't describe to you what that talk was like. Maybe you know. Did you have that yourself, ever? That talk? It's more than just that you're similar… it's like, you react together like a couple of… chemicals or something… you wrench each others' eyes open.

I wish I had a whole new language to tell you what that afternoon was like.

We talked about his mum, of course. I had always sort of known things were bad, but I didn't know *how* bad. Does he tell you how bad, when you speak to him? He still downplays it. Even now, after all this time. Back then, I had no idea. I didn't know how much he was doing, to keep the appearance of normality, all this time we'd been hanging out, getting closer. Nobody knew. I told him about my dad and Lizzie's mum, too, and how it made me feel. It seemed unfair, when Dad had been so great that day. But I wanted to give Day something in return, and that was the best I had. He looked interested, but not shocked. *That's a bit fucked up,* he said. *D'you mind?*

Of course I mind, I said, *It's Lizzie's mum! She's married! She's awful!*

Yeah, but, if it wasn't? he said. *You know, I mean, your dad'll probably get married again at some point. Or get another girlfriend or something.*

I must have made a face, because he laughed and said, *They're just human, grown-ups. Look at them. They're as bad as we are.*

Are we bad? I said.

121

Well… we're a bit all over the place aren't we? he said, and kissed me for the first time.

Don't you love Lizzie? I said, afterwards.

No, he said. That's it. *No.*

Don't you love Nick? he said, but it felt like he knew the answer and was just asking for symmetry's sake.

We didn't go to mass that evening. Dad let it slide for once, even though I was supposed to do the Reading. We, the four of us, got a takeaway curry and watched a film instead.

Nick

They didn't turn up at 5.30 mass that evening. Can you imagine how it looked to me and Lizzie? I mean, we know now it was because of Damien's mum or whatever, but… think about it from our point of view.

I got there first. I was sitting on the radiator at the back, waiting, for ages. I got this sick feeling as time went on and it was about to start. Lizzie slipped in at the last moment. As the first hymn started up, I whispered, *You alright?*

She looked around and said, *Where are they?*

Your guess is as good as mine, I said.

She seemed upset. She seemed really upset. It looked from her eyes like she'd been crying. I don't know what had happened in between her blithe skipping home that morning and her coming to mass that evening. Something had, though. Maybe she'd just clocked on. Better late than never.

She said, *Nick, this is horrible. I can't believe this.*

I know, I said.

What are they doing? Why are they doing this to us? she said, and she was whispering louder and louder. I nudged her and said, *Shhhhh.*

I saw them together! she said, loudly. An old lady turned around and frowned at us.

What? I whispered. I gripped her arm. *When?*

So she told me. As she told me, she pulled up her sleeve and started rubbing her arm. I saw a huge bruise just above her wrist, just here. Big and angry, and all the colours of the rainbow.

I thought about it all, very carefully. The hymn ended and there was no Rachel to do the Reading, it was Father Patrick. I don't remember what the Reading was about. Then he started the homily.

I listened to the homily. And I was thinking.

And after a while, I whispered, *Lizzie.*

She looked at me.

Did you tell him to stop? I said.

She looked down at her arm. She didn't say anything.

I said, *I just, last night, I thought I heard you say no.*

Because I thought I had, at that point.

She was quiet for a long time. I wondered if she had just stopped the conversation. Then, *Yes,* she said. *I did say no.*

That was all we said. Seriously, that was it. Some people seem to think, when I've talked to them about it, that Lizzie and me got together and planned this. Like, it was some sort of conspiracy. Some sort of revenge. But genuinely – we were just trying to straighten things out. Trying to figure out how everything had changed overnight. I was trying to figure out what the hell had gone on in the next bed, while my girlfriend was staring over at it. All I did was ask her. Ask her if she said no. Because that's what I thought I heard.

We listened to the rest of the mass and then, when it was over, we sort of said we'd talk about it again soon. Hang out the next day or whatever.

As it happened, I wouldn't really see her again, at all. Not until years later. But how was I to know that? How was I to know what she'd do?

Father Patrick Creevey
I've always rather enjoyed delivering the homily. It's one of my favourite bits of the mass. I like to think that it represents

the same kind of bridge that the sacrament of confession does. Between the old and the new. The exclusive and the accessible. You remember what I said to you about confession earlier? Of course you do.

Yes. The point, you see – do stop me if you know this! – is that the readings, though delivered by a lay volunteer such as our charming Rachel, are the voice of God himself. Comes directly from scripture. It's all laid out in the missal what the reading will be each Sunday, so you, the priest I mean, can't exactly choose that. Where you do get to exercise a bit of creativity is in the homily, which the priest delivers, and which comes straight after the readings. I suppose it's a kind of glossary, if you will. Or maybe more like a critical introduction. Picks out key themes from the readings, applies them to current events and concerns in a way that people will understand. Not that people can't be trusted to take the message of a piece of scripture on board for themselves, but… well, often they benefit from a gentle nudge in the right direction. It's only natural. It's a professional opinion like any other. I mean, this is what I do. Did.

I write my homilies down beforehand. I spend the whole week writing them; just twenty minutes a day or so, but it adds up. I believe it's important to put the effort in. An ad-lib homily is a sloppy homily, and I hate delivering a sloppy service to parishioners.

Not that you don't sometimes find that, pre-planned as the homily is, it doesn't, ah, let's say happen to strike a particular chord with parishioners, which makes it seem oddly appropriate. Almost as if, some people have said to me, I knew what was going on in their hearts and was speaking directly to them. That's a nice idea, isn't it?

Anyway, the homily I delivered that Sunday, well, I remember it particularly well. I think that it was one of those moments then, when – if I can flatter myself for a moment, indulge an old man's vanity! – what I had to say struck a chord with somebody in the congregation. The next day saw a rush on confession from some unlikely places.

Would you like to know what I said?

Karen Cox

I remember the next day, the Sunday, much better than any of this other stuff you've been asking me about. Because that, *that* was when I clocked on something bad had gone on.

I mean, they didn't check out. That was the first thing. There was no answer when I knocked. The door was open when I tried it. So I went into the room and there was nobody there. And, well, I've seen some rooms left messy but it was like a car crash in there. Booze bottles everywhere and ash on the bed and the whole place stank of weed. And, well, then there were the condoms. Used. And blood on one of the bedsheets. (Sorry, but I'm just telling it like it is!) So, that was when I started to suspect there was no father after all. I won't lie, what initially sprang to mind was, for me, worse than what actually happened, in some ways. I didn't know about the girls, you see, we never saw them. But then I found the keys.

They were obviously a girl's keys. The key ring was pink, and shaped like a horse's head and that. So I would've known even if it hadn't had *Lizzie O'Leary* written on it. Next to the phone number. And then I thought, *Okay, gotcha.*

Silly little buggers should've at least checked out. They might've got away with it if they'd just checked out. But we needed the room keys back, you can't run a business like that, letting people do a runner with your keys whenever they want. And then I found big cigarette burns in one of the sheets, and I got pretty pissed off, I can tell you. And then I started to think, *What if we get follow-up on this?* It was pretty clear by then, even though we'd seen no sign of any girls, that there'd been some underage business going on. If the police got involved it could be seriously uncomfortable for us. Best-case scenario, there'd be some bad publicity. Worst case? Well, I won't say things like prostitution didn't come to mind, at that point.

I talked it over with Steve. *Best call 'em up,* he said. *Call the number on the key ring. Chances are you'll get the parents, and they'll take it from there.*

So I did. I did it that evening, the Sunday. About seven o'clock, it was. The news was just finishing on the telly. *Here it comes, Lizzie,* I thought, as I dialled the number. *Should've checked out, shouldn't you, miss.*

Kathleen

That evening, the evening that we heard what had happened, I was in the kitchen peeling potatoes. I remember, I was thinking about Lizzie. More about her than about me. It's funny that, isn't it, given that I had no idea what was coming that evening. We hadn't had the phone call, or anything yet. I suppose… the fact that I felt like I had gone so wrong, made me think about how I could stop the same happening to her. It was too late for me, but she still had a chance. Every day I saw in her, more and more, those little things about myself that I hated. Weak. Weak and desperate. I decided that there'd be no more running around with that boy for her. Or I knew what'd happen. I knew better than anyone.

When Paul picked up the phone and started stammering and looking at Lizzie, I *knew.* Don't ask me how but I just knew what she'd been up to. What a chip off the old block she was, after all.

But I never guessed that she'd deal with it the way she did. That she was capable of doing what she did.

Paul

The call came on the Sunday evening, when we had got back from mass. We were all in the kitchen. Kathleen was in a foul mood, one of those silent moods where you knew anything you'd say, she'd snap. So everyone was quiet. Lizzie was laying the table. Potatoes for dinner were on the boil. I can't remember what we were eating with them.

The phone went and I was closest so I picked it up. It was a woman on the other end, and she said, *Good evening, is this the house of a Lizzie O'Leary?* I remember that 'a'. As if she were an object, and as if there were lots of her in the world, and the caller wanted to know if we happened to have one.

I turned and looked at Lizzie, and I suddenly felt very wary, very cautious. But I had to say something, so I said yes, it was. Lizzie looked back at me, and the thought suddenly occurred to me that she'd hardly spoken all day, and I was scared. I was a bit scared. But I had no idea what was coming.

Who am I speaking to please? said the voice on the phone.

My name's Paul O'Leary, I said. *I'm Lizzie's father.* Everyone had stopped doing what they were doing in the kitchen, by that point.

The woman said who she was. I can't remember her name. And she told me she'd found the keys, in the room. In that damn B&B in Brooklands where it happened.

I said, no, she was staying with a friend last night.

She said that she wouldn't know anything about that but that the keys were at the B&B last night. That she had them in her hand. She jingled them, I remember hearing the noise, as if to prove her point.

I didn't know what to think. I thought, it would be some kind of trouble, and my first thought, straightaway, was how to minimise the hell that Kathleen would give Lizzie for it. I said something like, *Right, well thanks for letting us know,* and asked if I could come round and pick up the keys the next day. She said, *Well, it's not quite as simple as that,* and told me that they hadn't checked out and still had the keys, and there had been some damage done to the room as well.

I thought – well, I thought that I couldn't go into this any more without knowing what happened. I could see Lizzie out of the corner of my eye, sitting very still, with her head sort of drooping down towards the table. I thanked this woman for calling and said I thought I needed to have a little chat with Lizzie and I'd call her back.

I think that's a very good idea, Mr. O'Leary, said this woman snottily. *I'm afraid it looks as if there may, completely without our knowledge, have been some hi-jinks going on here.*

I said, *Well, yes, we'll see,* or something else suitably vague, and I took her number and said I would call her back either tonight or tomorrow. Then I put the phone down. *What was that about?* Kathleen said. She was standing with her hand on her hip and the potatoes were boiling over. I didn't say anything at first. I adjusted the phone in its cradle and pulled out a chair and sat down at the table. I would have liked to talk to Lizzie alone, but that's not how things happened in our house.

What's she done then? said Kathleen.

I looked at Lizzie, who was still looking straight down at the floor. I said, *Lizzie, that was a lady who said she's found your keys this morning. In a B&B in Brooklands.*

She didn't say a word.

I said, *Do you want to tell us something?*

She started crying.

Kathleen said, *What the hell were you doing in a B&B?*

I said, *Lizzie, I think you owe us an explanation.* I hate myself now, when I think how stern I was with her. She must have been so frightened.

Kathleen started off on one, *What were you doing, oh I think I can have a pretty good guess, what did I do to deserve such a daughter,* all this stuff. Lizzie just sat there and she took it. Then I noticed she'd started whispering, her lips just barely moving, whispering so quietly you couldn't hear a word in the bloody... noise coming from her mother, and I shouted, *For God's sake let her talk! Just let her talk!*

That shut her up, Kathleen I mean. There was silence except for the bubbling of the potatoes, and Lizzie drew in a big breath and wailed like a baby. A long, horrible wail. She said, *I didn't want to do it.*

Do what? I said.

He raped me, she said.

I couldn't believe my ears. *Who did?* I said.

Day, she said. She looked up at me.

I got up, I nearly fell over the chair, I remember, and ran around the kitchen table and I took her in my arms and held her.

I will never forget the next moment, when I looked up into my wife's eyes and saw her looking from me to Lizzie, and her expression said, *I saw it coming* and, *You don't believe this, do you?* That was the moment my marriage ended.

What were you doing there in the first place? In a B&B like that? she said to Lizzie.

I said, *It doesn't matter, it doesn't matter,* into my daughter's hair. Then, like I said, I took her hand and I got her coat and I took her down to the police station in my car. While she curled up on the back seat and cried because she'd been raped and her own mother didn't believe her.

Day

I have always been interested in synonyms. It seems to me that the way in which we use words to mean more than one thing are often delightful little windows into our collective subconscious. The term that stuck in my mind when the good doctor was doing his spiel was 'aspiration'. This word denotes the passage of something travelling into the lungs or windpipe that has no business being there. So, my mother aspirated her own vomit. Or, as I prefer to think of it, my mother's vomit aspired to her windpipe. The brain damage that ensued, the permanent paralysis of her functions, was the result of an unfortunate aspiration. I won't labour the point, but you see what I mean.

On the subject of words: although I hesitate to use such a hackneyed, meaningless brick of verbiage, I feel honour-bound to state that the Sunday evening was… lovely. There was that drained sense of exhaustion that follows a crisis, which food and friendship and comfortable surroundings can convert from a terrible feeling into an oddly delightful one. Rachel was extraordinary. Her father was extraordinary. Even my brother was behaving himself, only too happy watching the idiot box and gnawing on a naan bread. I knew, I felt, that we were in the eye of some sort of storm. Nick and Lizzie and everything, we'd have to sort that out at some point, and there were going to be social workers buzzing around Jordan and I after all this… but it was going to be okay.

Then the doorbell rang.

Michael went to answer it. He was quite a while, and when he came back there was a rather attractive blonde woman with him. I thought, *Hello Mike, you saucy old dog.* I must have been smirking somewhat. Then I saw the big bloke behind her. And then she took out a piece of ID and held it up to me and said, *Damien Brady?*

Yes, I said.

She gave my address, like a question.

Yes, I said again. I thought it was Mum. I said, *What's happened? Is she okay?*

She said, *I'd like to have a word with you please. It's quite serious.*

I looked around, at my brother, at Rachel, at her dad. *What about?* I said.

About what happened last night.

DC Eleanor Featherstone

It's funny what makes a lasting impression, isn't it?

Especially in this line of work. The general wisdom around

here is that you can't afford to get too caught up in the drama. You're there to find out what happened, put a file together for the CPS, bang, that's it. Next. Of course, it's sometimes tempting to want to start getting into the whys and wherefores, to speculate about the history of the thing and the personalities involved, but usually you just don't have time.

You do get the odd case though, which interests you more than the sum of its parts should. It's not necessarily the juiciest cases either. I've been in the force for twenty years this year, and I've been on rape squad and murder squad during that time and seen some pretty nasty stuff. Just the other day, for example. Got a call to come down to a flat where a body had been found – the lads thought it might be suspicious. The body was on the floor in the bedroom. The head – the skull, rather, since all the flesh had gone – was in the corner of the bathroom. It wasn't actually suspicious in the end. His dog was locked in with him. Bloke died, dog got hungry and started eating his face. Head must've come off in a bit of rough and tumble.

You'd think that might stick with you, but I doubt it will. Just part of the job.

But this one – this one you want to talk about – stuck. Occasionally I still think about it – even, what, fifteen years later.

You might think it's 'cause these kids were quite young. But we're used to that. But I don't think it was any of that, not really. I think it stuck with me because it was the first time I got given a case like this, and I wasn't happy with how it panned out. I must've been only, what, twenty-five or something back then, and you have, you know, you're keen and you have a certain idea of the way things should work, and… I don't really know what I'm trying to say. Just that it felt a bit sad to me. Taught me a bit about how things often go. So, the fact it stuck with me – maybe it's more about me than about them. The kids, I mean.

She walked into the station with her dad on a Sunday. Early evening. I didn't actually see her at reception. Looking back,

I think it was probably pushed my way because I was the only woman on shift at the time. Can't remember who was on the desk that night, but whoever it was came and got me from my coffee break and said we had a girl come down who said she'd been raped the night before. So I went off to get a quick statement. She was a pretty little thing. Looked nice, well brought up, clean and well dressed and everything. Stable background. Calm. Sober.

Come on. Of course this kind of thing crosses your mind.

Look, I'm not saying you care about some people more than others, or you believe whatever they say, or you treat them differently. But, okay. The most likely person to claim they've been raped is a prostitute. They are far more likely to be victims of genuine sexual violence than other women. But they're also often saying that they've been raped cause they haven't been paid. Right? So if the girl who walks through the door is dressed like a prostitute, you look at her with slightly different eyes. Not biased one way or the other, but you've got to be aware that whatever happened did take place under a particular set of circumstances.

It's the same thing, once you start speaking to them, if there's a clear agenda with the guy they're accusing. Like, if you say, *So he's your boyfriend?* and they say, *Not any more, he's just left me for this bitch down the road.* I'm not saying they're lying at that point, mind, or even that there's necessarily more to it than meets the eye, but you do go, *Ah.*

Anyway, I introduced myself and stuff, and took her to a private room to get an initial statement and examination. I gave her the choice of her dad coming with her – I remember she didn't seem too sure. Looked at him, and then back at me, and then he asked her if she wanted him to come, and she twisted her hands about a bit and then said *okay* in the end, and they both followed me through.

It wasn't a very nice room we had. This was back in, what,

'97, wasn't it? This kind of thing, sexual offences, was less of a priority back then than it is now, so we didn't really… well, we worked with what we had. Anyway, I took a dead brief statement from her, the who / what / where / when. Just the basics, so I could go and grab the bloke she was accusing.

First Evidence Kit. Piss in a jar, swab in the mouth, photo of any visible marks of violence. She was pretty untouched, apart from a couple of pretty nasty bruises on her arms. The one on the right arm you could hardly really see, but the one on the left arm was massive, all colours of the rainbow. Looked like she'd been held down. I took the pictures, asked her if she'd showered since it happened – she had, unfortunately, which is always annoying, from our point of view, I mean – and then we were done.

Her dad didn't say much. Just sort of clung to the wall looking awkward. Only time he spoke was when I took the photos. *What are you doing there?* he said. *Evidence,* I told him. Pretty obvious, that, wasn't it? Not the sharpest knife in the drawer.

Then I passed her on to the medical examiner for a more detailed examination. Reported the case to Bill Jennings, who was my boss at the time. He told me I might as well take it, seeing as I'd already started. Let him know if I needed any help, keep him posted. But otherwise, to just get on with it. It was a busy time, and that's how things worked. So that was that. It was my case.

Then I got one of the lads, Chris I think it was, to come with me, and I got straight down to Chesterton Close, to find the Brady kid and bring him in.

Paul

I said, as I was driving her home, I said, *Lizzie, that bruise.*

She was crying again.

Did you get that from him? I said.

133

She didn't answer me. I said, *Lizzie, love, you know...*

I don't want to talk about it, she said. *I wish I was dead.*

That was all I said about it. She needed someone on her side, didn't she? She couldn't rely on her friends. Even on her mother. Especially on her mother. I was going to be there for her, no matter what.

Day

About what happened last night.

For a minute, I confess I was stumped. I looked at the policewoman, and the policewoman looked back at me. I didn't want to look around at anyone else in the room, because I had not the least idea what was going on. And I didn't like it one bit.

Then it all fell into place. Somehow, *somehow*, the bosomy virago who ran the B&B had tracked me down, and wanted to bring us to task for the room. For not checking out. For the smoking. For the drugs. *Oh dear,* I thought. *Oh dear, oh dear, oh dear.* Damn the wily old fishwife. Damn my early morning urge for perambulation, and my haste to whisk Rachel away from the twitching, stubby fingers of Nick. I thought about holding my hands up and saying *mea culpa* just to defuse the tension. The weed wouldn't get me into too much trouble. A chat with an exhausted junior officer, a slap on the wrist and that would be that. But there was no sign that Rachel or the others had been implicated. And they wouldn't perhaps get off quite so lightly as I, given that their parents actually had some kind of moral high ground. So I sat there and thought rather carefully before replying. Which must have looked odd in itself.

This your dad? said the policewoman, nodding towards Michael.

No, he's my friend's dad, I said. *My dad's dead and my mum's in the hospital.*

She didn't flinch. *Well, I can talk to you about this by yourself, or in front of him. It's up to you,* she said, and looked at her watch.

Foremost in my mind was not wanting to get Rachel into trouble, so I said, *I think I'd rather talk to you alone.*

So we went into the upstairs bedroom. Michael's bedroom, where Lizzie had whispered in my ear, *Fuck me, please fuck me.* And the policewoman and I sat down on the bed, and she told me why she was there. She told me what I had done.

DC Eleanor Featherstone

What a funny kid he was. Dead serious. Dead polite. Lots of big words and grand sort of gestures.

Finding out what we did about him afterwards, his background and all, it made me wonder, *Where did you come from? Why aren't you like…* well, like his little brother, I suppose, who we already had on the system as it turned out, for nicking bikes. Must've been an inspirational teacher at school or something like that, which made him so… well, so like he was.

I didn't like him.

I'm telling you that in confidence, that I had that reaction. To a fourteen-year-old kid. I did not like him one bit. I remember being surprised at myself, because he wasn't, you know, rude or violent or anything. It was something to do with the way he spoke. The glibness of him.

I know what I mean. I'll think if I can put it a better way.

Anyway, regardless of this, I try to be reasonably polite and pleasant to suspects. No matter who they are, but especially if they're kids. So I sat him down and gave him the spiel, nicely. Just told him when she'd come in, and what the allegation was. That kind of thing. They often look angry, or very, very shocked if it's news to them. He looked at me for a long time. Then he started laughing. *Oh dear,* he said.

Well, I told him it wasn't a laughing matter and we'd have to take him down to the station. He just kept saying, *Oh dear,* and, *This is ridiculous.* I told him it was procedure and we had to investigate the allegation. *I wish I could tell you how ridiculous this is,* he said, *but I'm not supposed to say anything am I? You have the right to remain silent and all that.*

That's in the United States, I told him, *not here. But yes, it's probably better if you don't say anything now. We'll have a full chat down at the station.*

He put his hands together and held them out towards me. For a moment I thought he was praying, or pleading, or something, and I thought, *Oh no, this is going to be difficult.* Then I realised what he was doing.

I'm not going to handcuff you, I said. *You're going to be sensible and not try anything, right?*

He nodded, and put his hands back in his lap.

Come on then, I said, and got up. And then I asked him if he wanted an appropriate adult. His mum was in hospital. I asked if there was anyone else.

No, he said, and started laughing again. *There's no such thing.*

Father Patrick Creevey

I like to give my homilies little titles or themes – in my head, I mean! I don't put up posters or anything. The theme that Sunday was *Commandments: The Neglected Classics.* I came up with that particular theme, you see, because of what the readings were that week. I remember them well – unusually well. The First Reading was Deuteronomy 4, *Add nothing to what I command you: keep the commandments of the Lord.* Which is basically Moses telling the Israelites to take notice of the laws and customs that he's teaching them, but also telling them – and this is a quote – *You must add nothing to what I command you, and take nothing from it, but keep the commandments of the Lord your God just as I lay them down for you.* And then the Second Reading was the letter of St. James, coming in about as subtle as a sledgehammer to knock home Moses' point by saying, *It is all that is good, everything that is perfect, which is given us from above; it comes down from the Father of all light; with him there is no such thing as alteration, no shadow of a change.*

Now, I'll let you into a little secret. I don't particularly like either of those readings. Oh yes, we, the clergy that is, all have our particular favourites, and so of course we must all have our pet dislikes too. Now personally I feel like that kind of thing, with its focus on the immutable and the arcane, is just the type to turn my parishioners off. Make them wonder how something written thousands of years ago could be relevant to their lives today. It's a challenge to get them to relate to that. But then, I do enjoy a challenge.

So I started wondering about how I might make these rather dry-as-dust bits of scripture make some sense to the congregation. As it happened, I'd been thinking recently about the notion of responsibility. Boring old word, isn't it? Boring old thing, really. People, in my experience, don't like to think about their responsibilities at the best of times. They like very much to think about their *rights*, oh yes. People are *very* quick to talk about the inherent sort of quality of rights, as if they're somehow stamped into your DNA, free gifts that come with being born. But they don't like to think about the other side of that coin, which is the restraints that come along with being a social being, part of a community. They might see them as fetters or chains, if they were poetically inclined. *Why should I do this, or that?* they'll say to themselves. *What do I owe my neighbour?* Why *do I owe them that thing? I never signed up to this.*

In the last few years – you might have noticed this – politicians have clocked on to the fact that rights and responsibilities can be seen as tied up together in the way I'm talking about. Since, oh I don't know, mid-New Labour, the two words have been almost inextricably paired. *No rights without responsibilities, with rights come responsibilities,* I can't remember exactly what the Home Office slogan was. Clever of them, that. Only, the Catholic Church got there first. We'd been preaching that message for ages, or some of us had at least. In my own very small, insignificant way, that's the message I was trying to get across on that Sunday in August 1997.

Lizzie

D'you know what you have to do when you've been raped? Most people don't, I've found. They think you just go and say, *I've been raped* and they say, *Right, who did it?* and then go and nick them. No such luck.

It's like you... like you become this piece of evidence. Your whole body is this one big *thing* that they poke and prod and examine and take photos of and put in jars and cut up. They cut my fingernails and a bit of my hair and took spit from my mouth and I had to, they put a, they put something up inside me to get stuff from in there too. I had to take all my clothes off and they photographed me all over.

I know they've got to do it. I know they do it to help you. I'm not that stupid. But it seems so unfair that you have to go through that, when you've been through something already. It makes you feel like you're not a real person any more. Like providing evidence is all you exist for.

There must be a better way to do it.

Then I was allowed to get dressed and have a shower and they gave me a cup of tea, and some more people came and spoke to me. They called Day *the defendant*. They said it was all to get me justice.

I wanted to go home then. I almost wanted to just forget the whole business. But I said yes. What else could I say?

The fact is that I hate telling this story. That's why I don't like talking to *you* about it. When I tell it as a story, it sounds stupid. Only I know how it actually was, and it's the kind of thing you can't put into words, not really. When I tell it... I know it sounds like I'm a slag, or a pricktease, because I took part in the plan in the first place. But that was totally different. I was tricked. D'you think I would ever have done it, *ever*, if I'd known how things really were?

They asked me everything that night. I thought it would just be about that night, but it was about everything. The four of us, how we knew each other, how long we had been what they called *sexually active*. I realised that they were going to talk to Rachel and Nick as well, and maybe some other people, and I saw the whole thing just spreading out till it covered the whole world, and everyone knew what had happened. And I was sick on the floor. They were quite nice about it, gave me a break to go to the toilet and wash my face and stuff and then I went back and we changed room and carried on.

Rachel

I knew it was something to do with the hotel, of course, when the policewoman turned up. I thought she was there for me too. It was on the tip of my tongue to say something that would have given it away.

Not that it mattered too much in the end. It was all out in a few hours, anyway.

They came down the stairs after a couple of minutes, and I said, *Day, what's going on?*

He looked up at her and said, *Can I say?* And she said, *It's up to you, bearing in mind what I told you,* and he said, *Rape, Rachel. They're arresting me for rape.*

I just stood there and said, *What? What? What?* over and over again. When they left, I followed them out of the door and onto the drive. I stood and watched him get in the back seat of the car and close the door and put on his seat belt. I stood by the window, wanting to reach out and touch the glass, pull the door open, throw myself on him, do anything to stop them taking him away. But I remember, I was also suddenly aware that I was being watched. That we were all going to be watched. That how I behaved mattered.

I saw her looking at me in the rear-view mirror as they pulled away.

They drove down the road and round the corner. I still stood there.

My dad said, *Rachel, what's going on?*

Father Patrick Creevey

Of course, Catholicism was, in many ways, absolutely central to the New Labour project. We all know that now, do we not?

I'm a Labour man myself, actually.

You look surprised. Are you surprised? Ah, come on. You can try to keep religion out of politics, or politics out of religion, but it never, ever works. It's the same as trying to keep politics out of art. They're all the same thing, after all. They're all about people. About what we believe about ourselves and each other, and how we act upon it. I think it was Orwell who said, *The opinion that art should have nothing to do with politics is itself a political opinion.* Never was a truer word spoken. When books and peoples' mouths open up, it's politics that comes out, no matter what it might look like. It's religion too, though people don't think of it under that name.

And perhaps, if I may flatter myself, even when a parish priest like myself delivers a homily, it's his own humble piece of art.

Anyway.

I shall tell you what I said to my congregation that Sunday. I told them that I like to think there are two types of responsibility. Responsibilities towards God, and responsibilities towards one another. If we look at the Ten Commandments, I told them, we can see these two types clearly in evidence. The first kind: 'I will have no false idols'. 'I will honour God's name'. 'I will honour the Sabbath'. Et cetera et cetera. The things that we owe God in return for his love and protection. Now, these are the simplest kind of responsibilities, I think, to observe and to honour, though we all slip up occasionally. Where it gets complex is the second type of responsibility, those that we hold towards our fellow human beings, which are also, applied to ourselves, our rights. The right to life: the responsibility to not kill. The responsibility to refrain from adultery: the right to have our marriage respected. The responsibility not to steal: the right to rest easy about our property. The double-edged contracts that we each have with every person we meet. It was mainly of those that I spoke.

Some of these responsibilities are easy to fulfil, aren't they? Most people, for example – most people – seldom find themselves faced with the temptation to kill. Others though, are less clear cut. 'Honour thy father and mother', for example. Where does the line fall between dishonouring one's parents and following a path that may be different from that followed by one's parents? Are we bound to do everything our parents did? Exactly the way they did it? No. Each generation is different. *But,* I said that Sunday, *we are bound to consider the fruit of our parents' experience; to give it due weight; to respect what they have to say. And we would be wise, though we are not bound, to consider that although each generation is different, they are also the same… although perhaps not so to the sharp eyes of youth, which are frequently so* very *sharp that they can often only see things in black and white, and ignore the intermingling shades of grey.*

I got a bit of a chuckle there.

All these are important, I said. *All are central to living a Christian life, to attaining salvation. But if I were to be asked what is the most important commandment of all,* I said – and I remember this bit clearly – *the one on which all else hangs, the cornerstone of the well-lived life, I would say it is, 'Thou shalt not bear false witness.'*

Day

I never stood a chance.

In the red corner: Lizzie O'Leary. Flanked by her white-collar pa. Backed up by her manicured mother and her house with four bedrooms and a conservatory. Not to mention her be-suited, be-spectacled, fifty-million-quid-a-minute solicitor. Well-fed, well-groomed. Dull but delightful – easily led astray. *Such a nice girl.*

In the blue corner: Damien 'Day' Brady. Alone, isolated, teenage and horny, scrabbling desperately to keep his skeletons rattling around in the cupboard and stop them spilling out all over the ring. Said skeletons include suicide father, smack-addled alcoholic mother permanently on benefits (currently in hospital after aspiring vomit after overdose), and younger brother already on the books of the local bobbies. No other family to speak of. No income. No private solicitor. Good grades, but what of that? Scruffy, smelly, malnourished, unwanted, not our type of fucking person, thank you very much. BANG. *Guilty*.

As I sat in the policewoman's car on the way to the station – she had the decency not to try to chat to me or put the bloody radio on, for which I was grateful – I was mainly wondering why Lizzie did it. Why she said all this. I didn't know about anything then, you know! The keys or the homily or the fact she'd seen us. I had no answers.

I thought about a tiny sound in my ear, a noise I hardly heard, a breathy subtext to Bach's sad strings. But that… but that was nothing. She said nothing afterwards. She fell asleep in my arms. She clung to me when we parted.

I thought of our little tinny radio, and of Nick and Rachel in the next bed. For the first time I felt a tiny stab of jealousy. Surprising, that, isn't it, when I had bigger things to worry about? I thought of the knocks on their doors, which would inevitably come. I wondered what they would say.

Father Patrick Creevey
Thou shalt not bear false witness.

Now, why is this the most important of the ten? I asked them. *Because truth, my dear friends, truth and openness, are the great antidotes to all the sins of which I have been speaking today. This commandment, so often forgotten, so frequently flouted, does not simply forbid false witness in its literal sense, that of pointing at one's neighbour and saying that he, or she, did something which we know very well they did not do. This is false witness in a particularly concentrated sense, the sense in which it has worked itself most deeply into our* cultural consciousness, thanks to a number of excellent TV dramas (got another little laugh there), but it is certainly not the only sense. This commandment covers a multiplicity of deceptions and withholdings. It refers, of course, to the practices of lying to one another and lying to ourselves; holding things back, keeping things hidden away in the dark places of our hearts. Of not speaking as frankly and as candidly as we can, and rejoicing in the clarity of conscience, the lightness of heart, that this simplicity can bring.

This is why ours is a religion of love and of salvation rather than hate and damnation. No matter what one has done – no matter what one has thought – being open and honest can set us all truly free. It is our eternal safety net.

I'd like to illustrate this with reference to stories. Why else do stories, I ask you, my dear friends, always end with an explanation, with an exposition, with a confession, with the detective coming in and explaining the truth of the matter? And why do we human beings have such an insatiable craving for these stories, no matter what our age? Because there is a love of truth deep within all of us. We are all, in the end, as little children, who speak simply and openly, from our hearts.

That's why Jesus said, 'Let the little children come to me; do not stop them; for it is to such as these that the kingdom of God belongs'. When we all speak and think, clearly, openly, honestly, as little children; when we scrub false witness in all its forms from our hearts; when we regularly take the neglected commandments down from their shelf in our hearts, dust them off and examine them with reference to our own lives… that is when we will be saved.

DC Eleanor Featherstone

I got the names and addresses and looked them up on the system. They all lived on the same road. One of them was a Nicholas Gardner. The other was a Rachel Vincent. She lived at a familiar address – the house where Lizzie had told me I'd find Damien Brady. The house where I'd been to pick him up. I realised it must have been the little, dark-haired girl, the one with the handsome dad. Who'd been crying when I took him away, and stood at the end of the drive when I drove off, looking daggers at the car. Why was she crying, I wondered. What did she know? I remember thinking, *Christ, this is getting sticky.*

I had Damien Brady waiting in the station for questioning, so I couldn't go and bring them in, these other two. Nick and Rachel. I asked Chris to go instead.

Day

The remarkable thing about police stations is how much they really do look like they do on the television. I'm not sure myself that this is entirely helpful, you know. For the police, I mean. In my experience, it gives the defendant an inflated sense of their own importance as soon as they walk in. One feels as if one's the star. As if there's a camera picking up each facial tic, as if there are hulking, grizzled officers watching them from behind every mirror. *Go on, this is your moment,* the whole place hisses. *Your episode.* You expect the full, undivided attention of the officer dealing with you, as well as that of their sidekick and superior. You also expect some sort of unspoken mental connection, for your particular brand of criminality or plight to strike some deep hidden chord within them and cause them to ponder their own personal issues. You expect, also, a high-octane, wisecracking sort of dialogue, and edgy music at opportune moments.

Alas! Aside from how they look, police stations don't actually resemble the ITV dramas upon whose glamorous tit I suckled. Not one bit. They have the good sense to snip out all the boring procedure in the dramas. The *Name, Age, Address.* The *Got any drugs? Got any mental health issues? Want anyone informed? Want a solicitor?* The fingerprinting. The photographing. The swabbing of the mouth and the penis (which, by the way, HOLY MOTHER OF GOD). The clipping of the nails. The snipping of the hair. It all manages to be boring and rather horrible and dehumanising at the same time. With every click of the clippers or flash of the camera or nick of the swab, I felt oddly as if the great machine represented by the tired, sweat-patchy officers around me took a little piece of my self, one that I could never get back. Which tribe or race or whatever was it who thought photographs took a piece of your soul away?

Anyway, eventually we were all assembled in a smelly little room. Me, my foxy blonde friend and her pimply colleague, and a waste-of-air solicitor. They started the tape recorder.

The first question DC Featherstone, as I was being asked to call her, asked me was if I knew why I was there.

You told me what the allegation was against me, I said. *I assume that I'm here because somebody has accused me of raping them.*

She asked me if I knew who that person might be.

I'm guessing Lizzie O'Leary, seeing as she's the only person I had sex with last night, I hazarded.

She settled back in her chair, and crossed one leg over the other to show me the sole of her shoe. I remember it had chewing gum stuck on it, all blackened from the dirt. She was only young I suppose, maybe only ten years or so older than me, but I could feel she'd done this before a million times. So had her colleague. So, more worryingly, had the solicitor. They were all clearly thinking about coffee, and the kids' problems at school, and if they left the washing machine on, and did they have a cold coming. I felt terribly as if I wanted to say something to shake them all out of it.

Why don't you tell me what happened last night, in your own words? she said.

I looked around the table. This would have been a moment, in my police drama, where the camera panned around the table behind everyone's head, focusing in on each person's face in turn, finishing up with mine. *Thanks for that,* a voiceover sneered in my head, buckling with a wry laugh. *Good of them, after taking my genetic material, freedom and belongings from me, to allow me my very own words.*

I didn't give them my own words, of course. Nothing could be further from what I gave them. You, my friend, may flatter yourself that you have received this account *in my own words*. What I delivered to my captors was an account of what happened in *their* words. In words that they would understand.

DC Eleanor Featherstone

You could see that he was trying to become someone different in the interview. You know, I told you he came across as a little… well, a smart-arse, I suppose, is the only word. And then he just seemed to suddenly completely change for the interview. Not in a way anyone could complain about, mind. He sort of quieted down and sobered up. And it was all over pretty quickly. No fooling about or anything.

Oh, he said what you might expect. That he had never been under any impression that she hadn't consented. That they had been sexually active beforehand. That she had taken full part in planning these hotel shenanigans in the days leading up to it, and on the night had responded to his advances in a manner that led him to believe that she was perfectly willing to proceed with full sexual intercourse. That she hadn't said anything to make him believe that she wanted to stop. That she hadn't said anything afterwards. That they had parted on good terms. That she was lying. Et cetera, et cetera.

He was good. I'll give him that.

After I'd taken him to his cell and the solicitor left, I said to Chris, *What d'you think?*

Not much disagreement between their stories really, is there? he said. *Just whether she said no or not. Seems like we need to get these witnesses in.*

I mean of him, I said.

Oh. Right. Seems like a decent enough lad on the surface of it. Straightforward. Same old story, isn't it?

Mm, I said.

Bad background though, eh. We might want to bear that in mind. Get the social services to look into abuse and that.

Yeah. Good idea, I said.

What do you think of him? Chris said.

I didn't say what I really thought.

You know what? This case, the O'Leary case, taught me that why I wanted to join the force was to find out the truth. But it taught me, too, that sometimes I just wouldn't be able to find it; there were not the structures, not the tools in place to find it at all. Lots of people I'd interviewed before and who I've interviewed since then, bad blokes, nasty women… they can lie through their teeth, but they can't help somehow telling the truth at the same time. With their eyes, their lips, their fingernails, the way they sit, the way they pick their polystyrene cups. They have a truth to reveal; they just don't want to reveal it.

None of that with him. Damien Brady was a closed book, because he didn't have a truth. He was like, I don't know, like an onion. Made up of a million layers. But with no core. No heart. No discoverable truth. What he did have was a voice. And a good one too.

Her? She was all truth. Rawest thing I ever saw. But no voice. We didn't have the tools to help her say what she wanted to say. To be strong enough to… I wanted to help her. But I couldn't. It wasn't possible, in the end.

Rachel

Of course, I knew they'd come for me. Probably sooner rather than later. I was *dying* for them to come for me. Dad wanted to sit with me in the interview, but I said no. It was embarrassing enough telling him I'd had sex the night before. He didn't seem so surprised, though. He was very quiet, actually. You'd expect a dad to do some ranting and raving about the whole thing, or at the very least some hand-wringing. But it was like there was no fight in him. He just said, *But you're okay, aren't you? There was nothing like that with you?*

No, I said, *I'm fine. Honestly.*

And he didn't do it?

Rape her? I said, wincing at the word. *No.*

So she made it up?

I think so. I don't know, I said. *I don't know anything. I don't think she'd... I can't imagine why she'd do that. She loves him. She's obsessed with him.*

That's when the thought first occurred to me. That she saw. That *they* saw something.

Nick

They came round at about ten o'clock in the evening on the Sunday. I was just off to bed. I remember, I was in my pyjamas and cleaning my teeth. I was feeling pretty shit. I hadn't heard from Rachel. I was still thinking about the Damien and Lizzie thing too. Like, was that *rape*? I was asking myself the question as I cleaned my teeth and looked in the mirror. I thought about telling Rachel about it. I mean, I assumed she must have heard too, but I'd force her to think about it, to recognise him for what he was. Then maybe she wouldn't think he was so fucking fantastic. But this was all in a sort of weird dreamlike way. I had no idea what was coming. Not really.

Then my dad called me. I looked down the stairs and said, *What?* He was sort of tapping a rolled-up newspaper against his leg.

There's someone here to see you, he said. He looked a bit... confused.

I went downstairs and there was a policeman. And I knew what it was about. I knew. Straightaway.

They told me at once that I wasn't in trouble, but that they thought I was witness to a serious crime and all the rest of it, and that I needed to come down the station. So of course, I went.

Rachel

The policewoman said, *How would you describe your relationship to Lizzie O'Leary?*

I said she was my friend.

How would you describe your relationship to Nicholas Gardner?

I said he was my boyfriend.

How would you describe your relationship to Damien Brady?

We're good friends, I said. *Same as me and Lizzie.*

I was in there for a long time. Probably hours. There was this policewoman doing most of the questioning. I didn't like her. It felt like she was there to catch me out. There to pick holes in what I was saying, there to make me incriminate Day. It wasn't so different, you know, sitting there in that little bright room which smelt of coffee and disinfectant, to sitting in the little dark box I knew so well, that smelled of incense and guilt.

And, like being in confession, you had to be clever. To know the right thing to say and when to say it. But also, to make them think that you had no idea about what was the right thing to say and when to say it.

Of course, I said I didn't hear anything.

She is quite clear that she said no, the policewoman said to me. She was talking about Lizzie, of course. In fact, she seemed to have very little interest in what I had to say except as a kind of Polyfilla for what either Day or Lizzie had already said. And then she added, which she did after every statement I made that didn't exactly tally, a hundred per cent, with what Lizzie had come out with, *Are you saying that she's lying?*

No, I knew to say, *I don't think she'd lie, exactly.*

Why didn't I say she was lying? Well, isn't it obvious?

She asked me what I meant, and I said I thought maybe Lizzie was confused in her own head, mistaken. But I couldn't resist adding, *She sounded as if she was enjoying it.*

Did you see him at any point hold her down by her wrists? was the next one.

No, I said, *Definitely not.*

I remembered a doctor's eyeline, and Lizzie pulling the thin sleeve down over her wrist, to hide what was already there. Already there, a few days ago.

That was the important bit.

Nick

They said, *Did you at any point hear Lizzie O'Leary say anything while she and Damien Brady were in the other bed together?*

I said, *I heard some noises, yes.*

What did she say? said the policelady.

I didn't know what to say. I looked around and I thought about what I heard and the moment I heard it, and looking over and seeing…

I thought she said no, I said.

What do you mean, you thought? said the policelady, but in a nice way.

I think I heard her say no. I said.

How sure are you? She said. *This is very important.*

I'm ninety per cent sure she said no, I said.

That was the first interview.

Rachel

No, hang on. There was another important bit.

She asked if Nick and I had sex.

I asked if that was relevant.

She said it might be.

I said I'd prefer not to answer the question.

She said it would be very helpful if I could.

We stared at each other across the table, and I thought. I thought very hard. You'd be surprised if you knew what I thought about at that moment. It's not what you'd expect.

No, I said. *We didn't in the end. Just kissing and stuff, you know.*

Nick

Of course I said we had sex. That was the truth. Or that's how I saw it at the time.

DC Eleanor Featherstone

So that was where we were.

We had these four, all saying different things. The victim, and one witness, says she said no. The defendant, and the other witness, says she never said no. Then, as if there wasn't enough contradiction, out of the other couple, one of them says they had sex and the other one says they didn't. Compromises the reliability of at least one of them somewhat, doesn't it?

It was gone midnight on Sunday, so we sent the two witnesses home, under strict instructions not to contact one another – or the victim or defendant. Damien Brady had to stay in the cells overnight, but we'd be starting again bright and early – we only had twenty-four hours until we had to bail or charge him. So I went home for some kip myself. Set the alarm for six thirty. I thought I'd be out like a light, but I surprised myself.

Father Patrick Creevey

I won't deny it. When I said, just now, that I found sometimes people told me that my homily seemed to speak directly to them, as if I knew what was in their hearts… I had this particular case in mind.

That Monday, as I hinted earlier, I had a bit of a rush on confession. A most interesting morning, it was.

Oh, I can't tell you what passed in those confessions. No, no, no. Not at all. That's the most important thing about confession, you understand. The sacramental seal is utterly inviolable in this respect. It's absolutely forbidden for a confessor to betray a penitent in words or in any manner or any means. That's a direct quote from the Code of Canon Law, by the way, but I think it does the job pretty well. In short: you're wasting your time.

Sorry. I don't mean to sound stern. It's natural to want to know the truth. That's why you're here, after all. But don't you see, confession wouldn't work at all, if people thought I'd just go and tell everybody what they'd said. It would entirely defeat the point.

Still. That's the particulars. I suppose there can't be much harm in telling you, now all this time has passed, that it was Nick and Lizzie who came to me on Monday. And Rachel, of course, but not in the way she intended to. Why don't you ask them about it yourself? You seem to be having quite a successful time of it, for an amateur. They must feel comfortable with you. You never know your luck.

Rachel

I woke up on the Monday morning to rain. I made myself a coffee and then went back upstairs and sat up in bed and thought about how I was going to get us all out of this.

The ban on speaking to one another was the worst thing. I had to see Nick. I had to see Lizzie too, and that was going to be harder, seeing as I had no idea where she was coming from, but I had to see Nick first. To find out what he'd said. To find out if our stories matched up. And to deal with him. I had a good idea of how to deal with him.

I couldn't just go round to their houses, you see. I'd been expressly forbidden to do that, and I didn't know what might happen if I did. But I had to talk to them.

I got into bed and out of bed. I drank my coffee and I made another and I tried to think of what to do, how to get to them. I thought about manufacturing a disaster, carrying a fake message from my dad, sending a note, throwing gravel at their windows. But it all seemed too risky, and I was just about thinking of giving up, staring out of my window at the dull rain-sodden street, when I had my problem solved for me. I saw a figure jogging along in the rain, with his grey hoodie pulled up and his head down.

I saw him glance up briefly at my house. I saw him turn into the church car park, and then enter through the side door. Of course. It was Monday.

It was a free country. Nobody could stop me from going to confession.

I pulled on some clothes in a hurry. I left the house and crossed the road in the rain, and then I opened the door and let myself into the church. It was vast and silent and accusing, like always. Nobody else was in there. I walked down the aisle and looked at the altar for a moment. Then I went and sat in a side pew, with a good view of the confession box, which had the red light over the door meaning that somebody was in there, confessing their sins. I folded my arms and crossed my legs and waited for him.

Nick

I suppose I just wanted some… guidance. About what I'd said.

Is ninety per cent sure enough? Enough for something like that?

It seemed like every way I turned, I hurt someone very badly. Lizzie or Day, that is. It's easy to talk about being honest and open and all that, isn't it, but when it comes down to it, what if you don't know exactly what you heard?

I always worked my way back up to the same point in the end. That if I didn't know who to hurt then I should hurt Damien.

Because I was more sure that I'd heard her say *no* than that I hadn't.

But also because he deserved it. It's like Father Creevey had said, you've got to accept you have responsibilities. Responsibilities to those around you. To behave to them as you'd like them to behave to you. Well, he'd shown quite clearly that he felt no responsibility towards me. Or towards Lizzie. Why should I feel any towards him?

So, I suppose I just wanted to talk these things over. There's nothing wrong with that. Father Creevey was really helpful, actually. By the time I left, I was pretty clear on what I had to do. I left confession feeling better and started walking out of the church. Then I found Rachel waiting for me.

Rachel

It was on just about the same spot where we first spoke to each other that he saw me and stopped walking.

I said, *Hello.*

He looked delighted at first. I thought, *He's glad to see me, even now,* and I felt a kind of wringing of my stomach. Then he frowned and said, *I don't think we're supposed to see each other right now.*

I said, *Come and sit down with me for a second, I need to talk to you.*

He said, *I really don't think I can.*

I said, *Nick. You know, they could arrest you too.*

I've never seen anyone look so scared.

He said, *You wouldn't...*

I said, *No! No, of course not. But just come and sit down. I need to explain something to you.*

He sat.

I said, *What we did is illegal.*

He didn't say anything, so I said, *Did you tell the police that we had sex?*

Yes, of course, he said. *I had to! It's the truth.*

I said, *I told them we didn't.*

Why?

Cos I don't want you to go to prison, I said.

He opened and shut his mouth. He said, *It's not... they wouldn't... if you said you wanted to...*

I said, *It doesn't make a difference, Nick. Girls under sixteen can't consent. It's the law. You're a rapist. Technically.*

What do we do? he said.

I told him, *You have to go back to them and tell them that you made it up. Tell them you wanted to save face or whatever. Anything you like. I've already said we didn't, so at the moment they won't know what to think, and I reckon they'll just leave it if you say you made it up.*

He was silent for a really long time. A few people shuffled back and forth from the confession box, knelt at the front and said their penances. I pulled my feet up on the pew next to us. My jeans were wet and smelled musty.

Alright, he said.

Now for the difficult part. Because that had been the carrot, not the stick. I said, *Hey, I can't believe Lizzie said that she said no. Why would she make that up?*

He turned towards me. He said, *I heard her say no.*

What? I said. *You couldn't have done. She never said a word.*

She did, he said, *I heard her.*

How could you have heard her if I didn't? I said.

You did hear her, I reckon, he said.

She didn't say a word, I said, slowly and deliberately. I was willing him in my head, *Come on. Please get it. Please co-operate. Please don't make me do this.*

You just want to save him, he said. I didn't look him in the face, but I could see his hand on his knee, clenching and unclenching like a baby's. *Why are you doing this for him? Why are you lying for him? You should tell the truth!*

I closed my eyes for a minute to shut out the sight of his clutching hand. Then I opened them again and said, *Well, maybe you're right. Maybe we should all tell the truth. Maybe I'll go to the police and tell them we did have sex. Maybe that's the right thing to do after all.*

Silence, for a long time. We could hear someone fumbling with a candle at the other end of the church, lighting a candle to save a soul. Their money fell into the collection box with a clang.

Are you saying that you'll drop me in it? he said.

I'm saying that there are such things as white lies, I said.

He didn't say anything.

I continued. I tried to force myself to be dispassionate and clinical about it. I said, *Look, Nick. Sometimes you've got to think about the bigger picture. Don't get stuck on the little things. I think you should go and tell them that you made up that we had sex. And you should definitely tell them that you've been thinking about it and you don't think Lizzie said* no *after all.*

What if I don't? he said.

I said, *I think you have a good future ahead of you, Nick. Don't ruin it.*

He stood up. I could tell he was looking at me, but I couldn't look back at him. I never did again, really.

He started saying something. Then he stopped and ran out. I could hear the *slap, slap, slap* of his trainers receding down the aisle, and then the door slammed, and it echoed all around.

I thought about Nick on that spot; was it just a couple of months ago? Swaggering a little bit and saying *Alright,* and me turning around to see who he could possibly be talking to. And it was me.

The pricks of light that were the candles at the front of the church slid into long loopy lines of light, and everything dissolved.

Poor Nick.

Lizzie

I went to confession on the Monday afternoon. I was feeling awful. Just so awful. It was especially bad at home. My dad was trying to be nice, he always tried to be nice but... he was just hanging over me and fretting and I kept thinking of all the trouble I'd caused him and feeling so dirty that he knew what had happened. Like I'd let him down.

And my mum. Well, she was drunk. She was sort of wavering back and forth between not talking to me and coming to my bedroom and trying to get me to, what she described as, *take responsibility for my actions.*

When my dad heard what she was saying, he grabbed her; for the first time in my life I saw him grab her in a rough sort of way, and pull her across the landing by her arms into their room. They had fought before but this was worse than anything. And it was all because of me. I ran out of the house and I didn't know where to go so I went to the church.

Paul

It had finished already, really, but on the Monday it became irretrievable. With Kathleen, I mean. That afternoon, I found her in Lizzie's bedroom. Bent over her, holding her down, shouting in her face. Something about responsibility. I had never laid a finger on her before, but at that point I grabbed her around the waist and hauled her off Lizzie and into our bedroom. I sort of pushed her onto the bed and shut the door.

This is insane, I said, *You've gone crazy.*

We were in our bedroom. She was sitting on the bed, she was breathing hard and she was flushed. She'd drunk a whole bottle of wine at least that afternoon. Ah, the drink. Yes, that was part of the problem with her. Always wine, not spirits or anything. It wasn't the root of the problem or anything – the roots went far deeper than that. But it didn't help. It was never serious enough that she was necking vodka or hiding the bottles, you know. Just a glass or two of wine in the evening, every evening, and then *Ah sure, why not finish the bottle?* Over time, it would edge forwards to the late afternoon, then mid afternoon. By evening she'd be sozzled, but often so's you could hardly tell. She wasn't reeling everywhere or anything. Just angry. Stroppy. Sniping at Lizzie, for this, for that, for the other.

Usually I just tried my best to protect everyone, keep everyone together. But this was too much. I had never seen her this bad before. She was out of control.

I said, *For God's sake. She's been raped. She's been raped and you're treating* her *like the criminal.*

She's lying, she said. I remember, spit flew out of her mouth.

Why would she lie? I shouted. *Why the hell would she make this up?*

She said, *She's been all over that kid for months. She's been trying to sleep with him. If it was really rape, why didn't she tell us before the phone call? Before we found out about the keys?*

It doesn't matter, I said. *If she says it, then it happened.*

Ah Paul, she said. *You're just believing what you want to believe. What about that poor little eejit? What about his life being ruined because she's trying to get herself out of trouble? Tell me something. Just try not to be so blind for a second and tell me something. Where's the evidence? Did she fight back? Where are the marks on her?*

I said, *She's got bruises. On her arms.*

She looked at me and I looked at her. And she smiled at me, a weary rueful smile.

And I knew I had lost.

She said, *Ah, nice. Very nice. You think I'll keep quiet 'cause I'm ashamed? You think I'm that selfish? You really do, don't you?*

I said, *Don't...*

She said, *You know what? I know I've failed sometimes. But I'm always trying to help her. But you? You. You'll shut your eyes to a lie that could ruin someone's life because you don't want to stir yourself to tell her the difference between right and wrong. So which of us is more at fault, Paul, when it comes down to it?*

Lizzie

Bless me, Father, for I have sinned.

That's how confession always starts. I was there to confess. But I didn't know what to confess to, exactly.

Take your time, my child, Father Patrick's voice said through the grille thing. *There's no rush.*

I put my head in my hands and thought about it. Should I

confess to, you know, the sex? My part in it all from the start, as if I took some sort of share in what my mum had called the responsibility? Or should I confess about the way the story had come out, that there were some things I'd said that were sort of… not untrue but like an exaggeration? It was so tempting to fit everything into a shape that was neat, you know, that you knew people would recognise. Once you started making sure you were, what's that word, means you're really careful? Anyway, once you start being really, really careful about every detail – *scrupulous* – it's like you find you're actually weakening your own case. Shooting yourself in the foot, like.

Well, there are other people to do that for you, aren't there?

Rachel

Lizzie came later that day, just before the end of confession. And she was harder to convince than Nick. Nick knows what's good for him, which is in the end what makes someone smart. Means you can reason with them. Lizzie, not so much. She's never known what's good for her.

I don't mean that in a bitchy way. It gives her a kind of strength, actually. It's like – you must have had this – when you're trying to debate something with somebody who's not so bright, trying to get them to concede a perfectly simple point, just the start of your chain of reasoning, and they just keep saying *Well, that's my opinion, everyone's got a right to their opinion*, and grinning like an idiot. It's a total brick wall.

No, that's not fair, Lizzie isn't quite like that. There's that same sort of solidity, in that she doesn't like thinking about things so she sort of shies away from complexities, which makes things easy for her. But then, she is… pliable. With her, it's just kind of about what, or who, has made the most recent impression on her mind. You have to work hard to cancel out the most recent imprint, if it's a good deep one. Which was the job I was faced with at that very moment.

Paul

We both smacked her, when she was younger. Just discipline, you know. But then… it didn't stop with Kathleen. She still cuffed her or gave her a shake or pulled her around, and… I couldn't say anything. Because…

It didn't change the essence of the thing! The essence of the thing was that she was raped. If she said she was, she was.

It's natural that she would have said it. Even after everything, she was trying to protect her mum. It was easier, it was just natural, that she said he made her.

Lizzie

He said that God knew the truth of my heart. I remember that bit. That I could go and say some prayers, and go in peace to love and serve the Lord. That's how they finish it, you know. *Go in peace, to love and serve the Lord.*

Then you say, *Thanks be to God.*

I left feeling like I had dropped a massive weight. I knelt at the front and said my prayers. I whispered to myself, *I go in peace, to love and serve the Lord.* I kept saying it. It made me feel better. It was a beautiful feeling. I thought of, like, life up ahead of me, and a time when I wouldn't think about this any more.

And then I turned around to leave, and Rachel was sitting behind me.

Rachel

I said, *I need to talk to you.*

Well, *I don't want to talk to you!* she said. She was angry. It was the first time I had ever seen her angry. I remember thinking, She's *angry with me?*

Why not? I said.

You heard me. Leave me alone.

No, I said, and tried to take her arm. *I know you must be upset, but I've got to talk to you.*

Why don't you go and talk to Damien, she said.

They made no sense, those few words, spat out quickly like a bit of bad fruit. But they also made all the sense in the world.

Didn't change my plan, though. If anything, it made it easier.

I can't, I said. *You should know that.*

She didn't reply. But she didn't walk away either. She just looked at the floor.

I said, *Did you just go to confession?*

What if I did? she said.

Did you confess to making the whole thing up?

No! She said. She said it too glibly, too quickly. *You don't know what you're on about.*

I said, *Lizzie, how could you do this?* The church was empty except for us, so I raised my voice a bit.

I didn't make anything up, she said. *I told the truth.*

Then why the confession? I said.

She just looked at me, and didn't say anything.

Well? I said. *If he did rape you, and if you haven't lied, what's there to confess?*

It's none of your business, she said.

I said, *Lizzie, he'll go to prison.*

She said, *Stop it! It's… he shouldn't have done it. It's nothing to do with me. I've said what happened. Leave me alone.*

I said, *I don't know what mumbo-jumbo they've been feeding you in there. But this isn't okay. You're lying.*

It's not a lie, she said.

Nick and I will say it's a lie, I said. *The three of us will be saying it's a lie in court. Because it is.*

She looked at me, baffled. I don't think it had actually occurred to her that she'd have to go to court.

Also, I said. *Those bruises.*

She looked down at her arms, covered up as always. She pulled the sleeves down over her hands with her thumbs.

I know where you got those, I said. *I know it wasn't Day. If you say it was in court, I'll say you're lying.*

She looked around. At the confession box, and down at her arms, and back at me. And she said, *I don't...* Then she started crying.

There it was. I went to her and got her hands. I said, *Lizzie, look at me. I'm saying this to you as a friend.*

You're not my friend! She said, *You only, like, stole my boyfriend!*

Can you go through this by yourself? I asked her. *With everyone saying you're lying? You were confused, I get it. But you're talking about ruining his life. And whatever he says to you in that little box about how God knows the truth and you don't need to worry, just confess to him and say a few little prayers and then you can 'Go in peace to love and serve the Lord'* (I couldn't help myself doing a silly voice) *— it's all bullshit. The people you need to be confessing to are down at the police station.*

She shook her head and said, *I can't, I can't.*

I said, *You can. You have to. If you care about him, you'll tell them.*

She pulled her hands out of mine, quite roughly, and took a couple of steps back and sort of brushed herself down. Then she said, *I have to go.* And she turned and walked out. She didn't run, like Nick. It was all quite dignified, really. I sat down at the front of the church. I'd been in there all day watching people scamper back and forth, in and out of that box. I was cold, and aching from sitting on the pew. I closed my eyes, and thought about what I'd just done. I didn't ask for forgiveness.

Then I heard a door slide open. The priest came out of the confession box, and of course he'd heard it all.

Paul

We were sitting side by side on the bed. It was the first time we'd ever got it out in the open.

Do you want *her to say where she really got them, then?* I said to Kathleen.

I don't know. Maybe, she said.

They'll want to talk to you then, probably, I said.

Well, maybe they should, she said.

Why not leave it? I said. *It could have been him. It was him.*

This is over, isn't it? she said.

I just said, *Yes.* There was all there was to say.

Rachel

He said, *Hello, Rachel. That was quite something.*

I was sick of him. Sick of his twinkly little eyes and his soft slimy voice, and sick of everything he stood for, that had landed us all in this mess. It was like all the hate that had been boiling away inside me for years, for the priest and the churchgoing zombies, all narrowed into one hard sharp point. *It was a private conversation,* I said.

I'm afraid there was just a curtain in between me and you, he said. *I really couldn't help overhearing. Are you here for confession?*

No, I said.

Seems like there's a lot on your mind. You may find it useful perhaps, he said.

I ignored the offer. I said, *Did Lizzie tell you she lied about what happened?*

He just looked at me and smiled a little smile.

Well, did she? I said, shouting a bit.

Rachel, Rachel, he said in that horrible chuckly little way of his. *You know better than that.*

This is a crime! I shouted at him. *A proper crime! Do you have any idea what's happened?*

Everything that people tell the priest in the confessional is bound by an oath of silence, Rachel, he said.

You should go to the police, I said.

I'm sorry, dear, I'm afraid I can't talk about this anymore, he said. *I've got plenty to do, so if you'll excuse me. I'll see you on Sunday.* And he turned his back to go into the vestry.

There'll be no more priests after you, I said. He turned and looked at me.

You, I said, *think you know how the world goes. But you don't. You're getting left behind.*

I'm sorry? he said.

Look at your 'flock', I said. *I know when you stand up there and look out at the congregation, exactly what you see. I've stood there myself. You know what I see when I stand there?*

Do enlighten me, he said. No twinkliness now.

Grey hair. White hair. Bald heads, I said. *The young people — us — we all sit at the back. We can't wait to get out of the door. We can't get out fast enough. And as soon as we're eighteen, we'll leave and never come back.*

I'm sorry you feel like that, he said. *But I'm afraid not everybody thinks the same way you do.*

You may be able to manipulate someone like Lizzie for a bit, I said. *Convince her she's committing a sin by being normal, that she can save herself by ruining someone else's life. Just shrug your shoulders and say,* Oh well, say a few Hail Marys and leave the rest to God, you'll be fine! *But not most of us. We don't think that. We don't believe in you.*

I felt a fierce kind of satisfaction when I saw his face. Like I'd stamped on a pane of ice on a puddle and smashed it, and could see the brown water beneath. *Go home,* he said.

I just stood there.

Go home, he said again.

I still stood there. We stared each other out for a long moment, and then he broke eye contact, and turned, and swept off into the vestry.

Father Patrick Creevey

Poor Rachel. So angry! And so unsure why.

She's clever, I grant you. I was a little shocked when she lashed out at me like that, because if she wanted to hurt me then that was a remarkably astute way to do so. Every priest walks around bent beneath the knowledge that people don't care like they used to. But then, necessity is the mother of invention as the old saying goes, and sometimes it takes these trials for us to think of new ways to do things, new ways to keep people interested. Keep them praying. Keep them hoping. Realising their responsibilities to one another.

I flatter myself that I do that anyway. I didn't need Rachel Vincent to tell me.

After everything, can you figure out why she hates the Church like she does? After all, if she really didn't care for it at all, would she not just happily move on with things, instead of going on about it the whole time? Perhaps it's because she recognises that faith has found a home in her. And she hates that. Oh, she calls it by a different name. But then, what's in a name? The difference is that hers is a lonely devotion, and perhaps a more testing one too.

DC Eleanor Featherstone

Well, as it happened, it all finished that day. The Monday. In the end, it lasted less than twenty-four hours.

First the boy Nick came in, must have been at about midday.

It didn't last long. He looked wrung out. The first time, the first interview, this kid Nick had been much like you expect witnesses to be. A bit self-important, a bit serious, but there's this little streak of submerged excitement. The same emotion that makes people rubber neck when they drive past the site of a car crash. But writ large. Because they're not just looking. They're creating a future for someone. All-powerful. Most witnesses are quite pleased with themselves.

This time, he was scared.

He said, *I've been thinking, and I want to change what I said yesterday.*

Okay, I said, and I started the tape recorder, and did all the preliminaries. *Go ahead then,* I said. *What do you want to change about your first statement?*

Well, I've been thinking, he said. *And I don't think Lizzie did say no after all. I think I was mistaken.*

I didn't say anything for a while. Let him carry on, let him draw himself out. The tape recorder was a big old clunky thing back then, and you could hear the tape winding in a scratchy sort of way.

Did you hear me? he said, finally. *She didn't say it.*

But you were so sure about it yesterday, I said. *Ninety per cent sure, you said. What's changed your mind?*

I just think... I don't think she said it, he said. *I was mistaken. It was just a mistake.*

I told him it was a crucial point of evidence. I asked him if he was sure he wanted to change his mind.

Yes, he said. *I was confused yesterday. But looking back on it, I'm sure that she didn't say* no.

Then he said he wanted to change something else in his statement.

What's that, then? I said. But I think I already had a good idea what he was going to say at that point.

I – he fiddled around a lot at this point – *I didn't have sex with Rachel.*

Oh, really? I said. And I thought, *Clever boy, clever boy. Who's got to you then?*

I said, *And what's changed your mind on that, Nick? Were you confused about that yesterday too, d'you think?*

No, he said. *I'm really sorry. I made it up.*

So you lied to a police officer in a rape case? I said.

I didn't think it was important, he said. *I was embarrassed, I wanted to save face, okay? I'm telling you the truth now in case it is important. Plus I know she'll tell you we didn't, and I don't want her to think I'm a knob. So, yeah. We didn't have sex. That's the truth.*

I said, *Has anyone told you to change this account?*

No, he said.

Are you sure?

Yes.

You haven't seen any of the others? Lizzie or Rachel? Since yesterday?

No.

Are you lying?

No.

Alright, Nicholas, I said. *Is there anything else?*

No, he said.

Okay. Well, we might need to call you back in for questioning. You've given two very different accounts, so it's possible we'll need at some point to get to the bottom of why they're so different.

Alright, he said, *But I won't be changing again. This one's the truth.*

I sent him away. I was keen to get back to Brady, and I thought at that point we'd definitely cross paths again. Because he was obviously lying.

The Nick Gardner evidence complicated the case, but it wouldn't have affected it too much. I mean, it'd just go on the file, but there'd still be enough to go to the CPS and it's probable they'd decide to take it to court. Couldn't afford not to.

But as it happened, I'd never see him again.

Rachel

You're probably wondering how I knew that.

The fact it was illegal, I mean. That it was rape on the boy's part to have sex under the age of sixteen, even if you were both that age. It's not the kind of thing your average fourteen-year-old knows, really, is it? Or is it? I don't know. Maybe everyone knows it. But the others didn't. And I did.

Creevey told me.

He mentioned it in his homily one day. One day when I was younger, before any of this happened, before I even knew

Day and Nick and Lizzie. He was talking about innocence, and childhood, and all that shit. And he was trying to link up religion and politics. He's always bloody doing that. And this time round, he was talking about how temporal law reflects God's law and all that, and he brought this up as an example.

Because I listen. Oh, make no mistake about that. I've always listened.

Do you know where the word 'propaganda' comes from? It comes from the Latin title of the Congregation for the Evangelisation of Peoples, which is a Catholic body that exists to extend the reach of the Church. Its Latin name is '*De propaganda fide*' – literally 'for spreading the faith' – and it became known as simply 'Propaganda'.

Fun fact.

Paul

I betrayed her that afternoon.

I was trying to do the right thing, of course I was. I can say that all I want, and it's true, but that doesn't mean it wasn't a betrayal.

She had gone out somewhere, that afternoon. I was worried. I didn't know where she'd gone, and Kathleen said she didn't know either, though she had plenty of ideas of course. She was out for a long time, and when she came home she went straight up to her bedroom and wouldn't speak to us.

I went to talk to her. She was lying on the bed. I sat next to her and stroked her hair. I kissed her cheek, like Judas.

I told her to tell the police about the bruises. Where they came from. God forgive me, I thought it would *help*! I thought it might damage the rest of her case… if they could tell that he hadn't made the marks, if they traced them back to us. To Kathleen. It was natural she, Lizzie, would let them think they were his work at first, of course it was. But they would eventually, I thought, incriminate her. Brand her unreliable, even a liar. And then, what kind of family would we look? They might even think we had told her to accuse him. To cover up our own goings on.

I thought if I could just get her to be precise about the truth – to say only exactly what surely happened.

I was a fool. It didn't matter who gave her the bruises. Her having them was the truth of the matter.

I had no way of knowing what she would go and do.

DC Eleanor Featherstone

I was looking forward to speaking to Rachel Vincent again. I don't think I've mentioned her, yet. If I had to sum up the impression she made on me, though, I'd say, *Not half as smart as she thinks she is.*

But then, smart enough, as it turned out.

I never got the chance, you see. Because Lizzie O'Leary came in that afternoon at about quarter to three, and said she wanted to drop the allegation altogether.

She was by herself. No dad this time.

I remember the scene very well. We were sitting in a room with a table and two plastic chairs in. I had sort of moved the chairs out from around the table further into the middle of the room, so we sat facing each other with just a yard or so in between our knees. I don't know why I did that. It's not standard practice. I suppose one of those workplace psychologist people would say I was trying to get myself close to her or something. Make her feel like the rape wasn't standing between us.

She was wearing a pink hoodie and jeans and her hair was in a ponytail. She had that very bright-eyed look of somebody who had been crying but had covered it up very recently and very carefully with mascara and stuff. I had a very strange impression of suffering, looking at her. Usually people describe suffering in particular ways, you know. Clichés. They say somebody looks crumpled up like an old paper bag, or caved in, or something like that. An idea of collapsing into yourself. But she… she gave me almost the opposite impression. As if she'd been sort of strung out by what she was going through. Spread thinly. She wasn't *there*. She was sort of diluted.

She said, *He didn't do it. Can we stop it all now?*

What d'you mean? I said. *Why do you want to drop it?*

I made it up, she said. *I made it up that I told him to stop.*

It was the second time I'd heard this in a few hours. As I had with Nick, I sat there and let her stew, and hoped she'd give something away. But as I sat there, twiddling my pen, I realised I couldn't sit there indefinitely because I was starting to get angry.

Why on earth would you do something like that? I said.

I don't know, she said.

Or is it now that you're lying, Lizzie? Tell me truthfully — has somebody told you to say this?

No, she said, *I made it up in the first place.*

Right, I said. *Why?*

I don't know, she said dreamily.

We sat in silence for a bit. I tried to think what to do. But there was only one thing to do.

Well, I said. *This has been a massive waste of police time.*

Sorry, she said.

I wasn't convinced she had made it up. Not at all.

But, if the defendant says she didn't say no, and the two eyewitnesses say she didn't say no, and then the supposed victim herself says, *Actually, yeah I didn't say no…* what have we got to go on?

Can I go home now? she said.

I said, *Yes, but I'll be in touch soon. I don't know what this will mean for your case. I'll have to talk to my superior and see. We may still prosecute, we may not.*

Then I went to see Bill Jennings.

It was over in about forty-five seconds. He was pretty stressed about something else. The office was a tip, the phone was ringing off the hook and people were popping their heads in and out telling him things or asking for them. He was in no mood to sit back and think about the subtleties, put it that way.

He said, *So essentially, they're now all saying the same thing?*

Yes, I said. *But look Bill, I don't like it. Seems too convenient. I think someone's been scaring them maybe.*

Got any proof?

Not exactly, I admitted *Nothing explicit. Not yet. But I think we should pass what we've got on to the CPS and let them have a look at it. Make some more enquiries.*

Let me tell you something, Ellie, he said, rifling through some papers. *Seven out of ten rape accusations end like this. Hasn't even been twenty-four hours, has it? Drop it.*

But, I mean, according to the legislation it's still USI. They're both under sixteen.

That's a very different thing to rape, he said. *And since when do we chase kids having consensual sex?*

But the legislation says – I persisted.

I know what the legislation says, Ellie, don't chuck the book at me. But look me in the eye and tell me you think it's a good use of bloody overstretched police and CPS resources to prosecute kids for fooling around with each other if nobody, I mean nobody, is now saying that there wasn't full consent?

I couldn't really say anything to that. I said, *I just feel like there's something not right about this.*

Noted. But I'm afraid we've got to drop it. We've got shootings up in Whalley Range, the press all up our arse about abuse in that care home in Wythenshawe, and real rape down in Longsight. I need you on that. Not faffing around with bloody Dawson's Creek here over in Sale.

I was going to have one last go but he just glared at me and said, *Less of the face. Go on, get out.*

He was a good boss in general. But that was how things were. Not enough time, not enough officers. If the victim can't even get her story straight, she's got no chance.

That's the problem with rape. That's always been the problem. At least with murder, there's a body.

Day

I don't generally dwell on the time I spent in that place. Never when I tell people the story. And even in my own mind, where as you know these things constantly rattle around on high spin, all the time. Even there, as little as possible.

Perhaps you think it's obvious why not. The grimness, the cold, the Spartan sparseness of the place? The feeling of confinement? The horrible scratchy babygro they made me wear? None of that bothered me very much, to be honest. As I said earlier, there was a pervasive sense of unreality attached to the whole experience that was not entirely unglamorous. I would have been disappointed, I think, if it had been more comfortable.

And I told you, I think there's actually quite a lot to be said for confinement.

No, the main thing I hated was that there was nobody to talk to.

I asked to see my solicitor a lot. They couldn't stop me doing that. To ask about points of law, count up the number of ways in which I was guilty, make risqué quips about imbecility and try to provoke some sort of mobility in the flinty shingle of her lower face. She left me for the evening eventually, impervious to the most acute emotional blackmail I could muster. So, all night, I asked repeatedly for coffee or tea – word to the wise, you're allowed as much of that as you want – and endeavoured to engage the dogsbodies who brought it in badinage. I suspect that by Monday afternoon, the lot of them were beginning to hate me.

So my main response when she came to get me for the second time that day was relief. Relief that I'd have someone new to talk to. I started babbling away the second she walked in. So I hardly took it in when she said it. It came to me with a sort of delay, like a long distance telephone call.

I remember the exact words. Well, you would, wouldn't you?

Lizzie O'Leary's dropped all the charges against you. We won't be taking any further action. You're free to go.

Why? I said.

Why what? she asked. *Why has she dropped the charges?*

Yes, I said. *Why would she do that?*

She looked at me in a way I didn't like. It made me uncomfortable. She said, *Your guess is as good as mine.*

Bill Jennings

Sorry, what? Brady. O'Leary. No, no idea.

Sorry.

Oh, Ellie Featherstone. Yes, of course I remember her. Done very well, she has. Last I heard, she was with the Met now. But she started off on my watch, in Sale. Talented officer. If a bit... well, never mind.

Well, all I mean is, she was always very career-focused. Not that that's a bad thing. It's a good thing. And you know, we need more of that type in the force, so I'm not criticising.

I just got the impression with Ellie sometimes... it wasn't just that she just wanted to dot every i and cross every t. But that it was sort of a bit... personal. That there was something close to glory hunting going on there. She wanted every case she was on to be *the* case. Of the year, of the decade. Which sometimes made her a bit of a pain, if I'm honest. You'd have to tell her, *There's nothing to see here. Dead end. Move on. There's plenty of other stuff to do*. And she could get a bit mulish over something like that. Some used to call her a jumped-up college kid who needed to respect her elders and betters. Others called her worse. I always liked her though.

She ruffled a few feathers alright. Well, she became something of a specialist on the sexual offences stuff, which has of course started getting a lot more attention in the last ten years or so. Political pressure, and all that. She's been at the forefront of that within the forces. There was some very bad feeling down in London around the time of the Worboys case, an old mate told me, 'cause some thought Ellie had been feeding journalists things she shouldn't. It's not alright, that. Not alright at all. You should keep the politics out of policing. She needed to find that out back then, a bit. And from what I've heard she certainly needs to find it out now.

Father Patrick Creevey
Well, there you are. That's about the sum of it.

For whatever reason, little Lizzie O'Leary dropped the allegation. And they all went home, I'll bet, a little sadder and a little wiser.

I heard about it all. Not just in the confession box, but on the grapevine, you know, long before you came around to talk to everybody. Not much stays secret around here. Apart from what people tell me, of course. A whole lot of rumours flew about, some true, some not, and everyone had their own hero in the story, their own villain, their own little theory about what happened in that mucky little hotel room and whose fault it was, and why everyone behaved like they did afterwards. It seemed to be one of those topics that really get people fired up in the pub. And the post office. And the school playground. And even the church.

But then something else came along, as it always does, and it all died down and soon enough nobody really talked about it anymore. The only one who really brings it up these days is Damien Brady himself. Poor fella.

I still say, kids will be kids. They might be cocky, or scared, or bolshy, or prone to the odd fib. In the end, they're all kids. They want to be forgiven.

That's true of everyone, actually. We're all kids at heart, in that respect.

That's what I believe, anyway.

Paul

I only found out what she'd done after she'd done it. That she'd dropped the whole, you know, charge or allegation or whatever. Can you imagine how I felt? I wanted to get down on my knees and beg forgiveness. But how could I tell her that? Without making her feel even worse? That she'd messed up again?

She wanted to apologise to him. She wanted to go and say sorry to her rapist.

I wanted to get her out of there. Away, somewhere new. So I applied for a transfer to the Slough branch. Took a few weeks, but HR were helpful when I explained. And Kathleen and I made our plans.

We didn't get a divorce. Not that it wasn't a divorce in my mind – but that isn't the sort of thing we did. Not the kind of language we used. It was *some time apart*, or at the most extreme, *a separation*. Admitting to a divorce seemed impossible. Bigger and more disastrous than a marriage not working out. A whole life, a whole belief system, overturned. She wasn't ready to accept that. And if I'm honest, neither was I. I thought it would be easier to do it incrementally. In stages. Once I'd got Lizzie away. Started our new life.

Kathleen

His name was Liam. He had sandy hair, and green eyes that crinkled at the corners when he smiled, and he was taller than any other boy in the village. He played the guitar in church, and all the girls loved him. My friends and I used to talk about him on the way home from school, I remember, and I was always the envy of them all because my brother David was friends with him, and he used to come round for dinner at our house,

It happened at David's seventeenth birthday party, actually. He, Liam, kissed me when we all sat round the campfire, and then he put his arm around me and I sat there feeling, ah, so warm and lovely and protected. I still dream about it, you know, that moment.

Then he took me off for a walk. We went into the next field and that's where it happened.

Well, I got pregnant of course. I suppose you've guessed that by now.

He didn't want anything to do with me then, of course. Wouldn't touch me with a bargepole. My brother was livid. My parents too. I wanted to get rid of it, but it was... you couldn't. Not back then, not in Ireland. I was only fifteen, and I felt like my life was over.

Then Paul came along.

He was... I suppose... kind of a friend. One of Adam's friends, that was my other older brother, who was twenty-one and had moved to Cork by then. But Paul had stuck around. He was doing odd jobs, trying to save up to move to England. He had always been a little bit in love with me in a hopeless sort of way. And then he said he would, well, he asked me to marry him when I turned sixteen. Said he didn't mind about the baby. We'd bring it up as our own in Manchester and nobody would know.

It was the kindest thing I've ever heard of.

Just look at us now.

I ruined it. Because, you know, although he did all that, I didn't love him. Never did. I was grateful to him, I told myself I was lucky to have him, I dutifully kept the house, and I brought Lizzie up as best I could.

I was never unfaithful, until I met Michael.

Paul and I didn't get a divorce. I don't think either of us wanted it, really. At first, there was always the hope that things might have worked out in the future, at least on my side. That sometime we'd talk again, maybe when Lizzie had moved out and got her own family and come to right. That he would apologise, and we could start again.

It was only later on that I realised that Lizzie had always been the problem. It was my original sin I suppose, that terrible time when I was fifteen and I had to have a baby, which had always lain between us and never gone away.

I just wanted to make Lizzie understand. I wanted her to understand that this kind of love, this violent unholy kind of love is the enemy. It seems like salvation, but all it will do is leave you spoiled and cast out.

I was trying to protect her. I wanted to do anything, anything, to stop her ending up like me.

Paul

That's how a marriage ends. Maybe I should tell you something about how it starts.

I felt sorry for her. She was the only girl in a house of boys, and she was bullied to death. Sort of cherished as well, a bit, but also threatened and bullied and controlled by all these brothers who'd kill as soon as look at any young fella who gave her the time of day. She was trying to do what young girls do, going out in groups and giggling and giving lads the eye, just innocent stuff really, but where most girls could get away with it, she'd get beaten. Her brothers'd hold her down and her mam'd beat her. I felt terribly sorry for her. I wanted to help her out. I felt a strong sense of responsibility to her, like, *That one is mine*. I can't think of a better way to put it.

When all that happened with Liam Driscoll, bastard that he was, I was afraid for her. Seriously afraid. Her mam threw her out, she had to stay with a school teacher while nobody else was speaking to her. She had such bruises on her. I couldn't bear it. I saw a chance to help her. I'd've been just as happy helping her in some other way, mind, if I could've thought of one. But it seemed like the only option. And I didn't mind the thought of marrying her. I'd had my heart a bit broken a year or two earlier, and I didn't really anticipate getting to a point where I could have it broken again, or put together again for that matter. I just wanted a new start, a change of scene; I'd always felt like a little bit of an outsider in the village, and I felt like Kath was too, and so, sure, why shouldn't we leave together? And if she was having this baby, which she would of course, well, why not? I'd always wanted my own family eventually. It seemed like a good solution.

She said yes, of course. And they said it was mine then, and everyone enjoyed the lie, and we were married when she turned sixteen, just a month or two before her due date. And all those who were beating or berating her kissed her on the cheek and drank her health. And we left, and we never went back.

But, the feeling of 'my' that I was talking about before? Here's the thing. That feeling was a pale, sorry shadow of the feeling I got when Lizzie was born. When I first saw this little helpless thing, with her puffed-up eyes and clutching hands. Every part there, perfectly formed. So loving, so helpless, so dearly needing. I fell in love for really the only time, that very day.

Michel

We didn't move back to France as a direct consequence of all this. But I was offered a position back in the headquarters in Paris, and I won't say that it didn't feel convenient. I thought that Rachel had been through a lot. And it would have been difficult for her when the new school year started. Somehow it had got out, and everybody knew about it. And her friends… well, they weren't really her friends any more were they? I found it hard to believe that they might be able to just go back to spending time together, after all this had happened. I thought that a fresh start would be best.

I'm not pretending that it wasn't convenient for me too. I couldn't look Kathleen in the eye when I saw her. I stopped going to church, to parish functions. I didn't miss them. When I heard that Paul was leaving her, I felt even worse. I had messed everything up for her, I know that. But I didn't mean to. I never intended to hurt anybody. It just happened.

Rachel and I had a talk about it all, the night before we left the house. We sat in the living room and got drunk, properly drunk, together. It was the day after her fifteenth birthday, and the first time I realised she was becoming a woman. Not just a daughter, but a real woman, a person in her own right.

Not only that. She's become a very clever woman. She understands the world. That is to say, she has an understanding of the world that satisfies her. In my opinion, that makes her a clever woman. Just like my mother.

I wonder on my more maudlin evenings, by myself, if it's skipped a generation. This understanding, this satisfaction. I get jealous of the memory of my mother and the reality of my daughter, though I know that sounds ridiculous.

I just try to learn from them now. To shut up for a change, and to listen to what they have to say.

Nick

So, yeah. That was that.

It's funny, when you get into it, how much you start to remember. You start thinking in your old ways, using your old voice. I mean, I genuinely don't think about it often, these days. Too much else to think about, But talking to you's made me, I don't know, live through it all again. Silly really, how upset we all got over all that stuff. But everything seems so important when you're a teenager, doesn't it. Hormones all over the place.

Anyway, it all seemed to fade quite quickly afterwards. That's why it's a bit ridiculous that Damien still seems to act like it was some massive deal, like for years he was Manchester's biggest swinging dick or something. Basically the girls both moved away – Rachel's dad got called back to France and Lizzie's parents split up so she went somewhere down south with her dad. And we weren't really speaking to each other much, just because, I don't know, I guess it just didn't seem right to at that time, after all that had happened. So we all lost touch. And so then it was just Damien and me. He moved away from the Close because after all that stuff with his mum, him and his brother got taken into care somewhere in Stretford, I think. So then, well, it was just me.

I still saw him around at school. Damien, I mean. We spoke once or twice. But I made new friends and I'd realised by that point, you know, we didn't have much in common anyway. Never had. Suppose we'd just been thrown together by living on the same street and stuff. I didn't owe him anything.

Anyway, then, you know, life happened. I went off to Oxford, got my First, went and started working for Deloitte. Risk-management stuff, mainly. I enjoy it. Pays well, good benefits. Senior Associate by twenty-five, took promotion in the Manchester office and now I'm back here. Met Chrissy, got married. We're expecting our first baby, you know. Due in December.

I saw Lizzie again, once. This is actually kind of embarrassing, but – oh well, never mind, it's not a big deal – I sort of slept with her. Yeah, I know. Bit weird, eh? It was a strange evening. There was a barbeque in London. Friend of my flatmate's. So I went along, and who should I see when I walked through the door but her. I recognised her straightaway. She'd changed quite a bit – bigger, but it kind of suited her. Done up quite nicely – a bit obvious, maybe, but again, didn't look bad on her really. Anyway, I thought it'd be rude not to say hello, so I went over and we got chatting – not about the past, just about what we were doing these days, what brought us to London – she had come to the party with a friend who was dating someone, actually, it was a really tenuous connection, massive coincidence. And, well, we had a few drinks, and I don't mean to sound like a dick but she was all over me. All over me. I knew what she wanted, and it seemed rude not to. So we went back to mine.

I remember afterwards. I lay with her in bed. I watched the light around the curtains changing colour, and the birds were making a racket outside. It had been a boiling night, and the room was stuffy and she was pressed up against me and making it stuffier. I could feel the stickiness of the soft parts of her where they lay against me, and the weight of the bedclothes around my legs. I was drunk still. Really drunk. Sometimes I felt elated. And sometimes I felt horrible, almost dizzy, and as if I was being plunged back into that summer where everything went wrong and I realised you couldn't trust anyone. And I felt sick at the thought of what lay there in my arms.

It was a Sunday morning, and I went to church that day.

I'm happy now.

I ran into Rachel, you know, when I was at Oxford. I guess she's told you. I saw her on Broad Street one night. I won't deny I did a bit of a double take. She… well, she looked very chic and grown up, and I hadn't seen her for what, four or five years. I went up to her, we said hello, had a bit of a chat. It was nice. Bit awkward, but nice.

We did that thing where we said we'd go for a drink and swapped numbers. Never really got round to it, I think we were both pretty busy. We talked on the phone a lot though, over the years. I feel like we've still got some kind of a connection. I think it means a lot to her. You never forget your first, do you?

Lizzie

I am okay.

I saw this counsellor once. My dad paid for me to see her. Mainly she just wanted me to talk. I don't really like talking about myself, so we didn't find much to say to each other. The main thing she told me was that I was okay. And that I had to tell myself I was okay. She said that a lot. Almost every time I went to see her. I don't know how much Dad was paying her, but I thought, *maybe I'll go into therapy myself one day.*

But you know, the funny thing is, it did help. I did tell it to myself, again and again and again. I am okay. I am okay.

I am, you know.

I'm a nail technician. I really like it. I always liked doing nails, and make-up and that. And I'm good at it. I make a decent wage at the salon where I work, and I'm thinking about doing a course to become a Creative Nail Design Education Ambassador, which means I can teach other people to do nails too. I still live with my dad – my wage might be decent but it's nothing special. Not enough to buy my own place, anyway. I'm seeing a guy called Steve at the moment. He's nice to me. But not as nice as he was when we first started going out. Like I told you at the beginning, I'm realistic about these things now.

I could tell you about all the men there have been since Day. I could tell you about lots of other stuff. But I won't.

I saw him once more, you know, before Dad and I moved away.

I really wanted to see him. Does that sound strange? Even though he'd done what he did, and I'd done what I did. I just wanted to see him once more.

It was the dreams, you see. I dreamed about him every night. Sometimes we'd be behind the shed again, and I'd wake up with my eyes all wet and my hand between my legs. Sometimes we'd be in the hotel room and it would be amazing, it'd end in a different way than it really did. Sometimes it'd be the hotel room still, but I would suddenly look at his face and it was Nick I was with, or someone even worse, and I'd know Damien was in the next bed with Rachel, and I'd wake up shouting *No, no, no.* And sometimes we'd be in a totally random situation, like wrapped in a blanket in the middle of a forest, or in a car together, or something like that. I couldn't escape it. Every time I closed my eyes.

So, I used to walk around in front of the flats where he lived. I wasn't really supposed to, my dad didn't like it when I went out alone, but I told him I went to see Rachel. Then I'd sit on the wall, opposite the flats where he lived, and read a magazine and hope that he was watching me, and that he would come down to talk to me.

And once, he did come down to talk to me.

I had my head down reading the magazine, and I knew from the first flicker of movement out of the corner of my eye that it was him. But I waited till the shadow fell across my magazine, and then I looked up. He was standing a yard or two away. Not close. It was evening and the shadows were long.

We looked at each other for a long while. I wanted to say all sorts of things, but *sorry* was top of the list and *how could you* was next up. I opened my mouth and I was about to say them both. And then he put his hand to his mouth and took out the gum and held it out to me.

For a moment I was going to take it and put it in my own mouth. You know how it's like you're in a dream and you don't act in normal ways?

Then he said, *This is you.*

I must have looked confused, 'cause he said, again, slower, *This — is — you.*

Then he dropped it on the floor.

I'll leave you to work that one out, he said. *Good luck.*

Then he turned and walked away. I watched him go down the street. I saw him turn and go into Rachel's house, without looking back.

It took me a while to work it out, the flavour thing. But I'm glad I got it.

You know what's funny?

When he turned to go, he did sort of a big dramatic spin, and he stepped on the gum he just dropped. So he walked away with it stuck on his shoe. I thought afterwards that maybe he trod it all over Rachel's house. Or maybe it just stayed there, on the sole of his trainer, getting tough and black. And one day he'd see it and figure out what had happened.

Rachel

I was distraught about moving away. But there was nothing I could do. What can you do, when you're fourteen years old? In the end, I got used to the idea. And it didn't stop me sorting things out with them all, though it made it a bit trickier. No mobile phones back then, you see.

I got Lizzie to forgive me through grim, bloody minded persistence. After it was all over, before Dad and I moved, I went round to her house every day. Her mum was never there, or I never saw her at least. Her dad always let me in. I guess maybe he thought it was good for her. Unlike some people, he didn't seem to blame me and Nick as well for what had happened. Just Day. So he'd let me up to her room and I'd sit there with her until it got too awkward and I had to go home. She wouldn't really talk to me. She was usually in bed, reading magazines. While I spoke to her she'd be flicking the pages, looking at the latest must-have shades of eyeshadow, reading about the heartbreak of soap stars. Silent.

When I moved back to France, I wrote her letters. I only got one reply, maybe a few months after I'd gone, saying that she'd moved with her dad to Slough, and her mum had forwarded my last letter on. It gave the new address. I took that as encouragement, and kept writing.

I never said sorry. I couldn't have done anything else, in the event, and I think it's kind of hypocritical to apologise for something you'd do all over again. I just wrote to her about my life. My new school, TV shows, holidays, that kind of thing. And asked her about hers. I always signed the letters, *Your friend, Rachel*. Because I think she needed reminding. Needs reminding.

I wrote to Day too. Of course I did. It was hard to keep track of him, but the difference was that he would write to me too, so he could keep me updated on his new addresses and we always found each other in the end. He wrote wonderful, grim, dark, funny, passionate letters, in spidery black ink, with fey little drawings around the edges. It got easier to keep in touch when we both got an email account, but I missed those letters when they stopped. Sometimes I ask him, these days I mean, to write me one. He'll ignore me for weeks, and then I'll find it propped up against the coffee machine or tucked under the remote control or something. He writes them on bills, on photographs, on steamed windows, on toilet paper.

I didn't keep in touch with Nick. I don't know why. Guilt, probably. I think I felt worse about him than I did about Lizzie.

Anyway, I always knew I'd come back to England, and then I could take it up properly again. Make things right. So I worked hard for my baccalaureate, and I got into Oxford. And once I was back over there, I looked them all up.

I ran into Nick by accident, actually, on Broad Street. He went to Oxford Brookes. We swapped phone numbers and said we'd meet up, but we never did. But then, like I told you, he'd ring me at night. Once every six months, like clockwork. I always took the call. Don't know why. Some kind of penance, perhaps.

He'd cry at me sometimes, you know, over the phone. Depending on how drunk he was. And he'd always ask me why I left him for Day. *I just want to know,* he'd say, over and over again. *I just want to know.*

Well, there's no answer to that, is there?

He can never quite decide, either, if we actually had sex or not. He goes through stages. Sometimes he'd want to talk about it in detail. *Our first time,* he'd say tenderly, as if there had ever been or would ever be a second. Then he went through a stage of deciding that we didn't actually do it, it didn't *count*. Because he didn't come, I suppose. He rang me up specifically once, to tell me that. I told him that it did count, or most people would say it did anyway, and he got a bit upset and hung up on me. But the next time he rang, he changed his tune again and decided that we did do it. That time, he told me – I think he meant to do this rather gently and magnanimously – that he had found 'someone special'. His wife, Christina.

He seems happier these days. Don't you think? Don't you think he's happy? I think he's happy.

Anyway. I was going to tell you – I went to see Lizzie, that first term I was back in England, at Oxford. She lived in Slough with her dad, and it wasn't far.

I went to see her on a day in November. We met at a Starbucks again, and had a Frappuccino, just like that day in Manchester, just off Piccadilly Gardens, when she told me she hated to tell her story. She was twenty minutes late, and when I saw her coming through the door I wasn't even sure if it was her. She'd got fat. And I'd got thin. Funny, that. She was still beautiful, though, in a robust, corporeal kind of way. She has these long, flat tongues of highlighted hair, and nice teeth, and nice tits. You know the type.

It was… okay. We talked a bit about it all. The thing that happened. As ever, we didn't have much to say to each other. It's funny that you can have friends like that, isn't it? She told me about the legislation, emailed me the relevant bits because I disagreed with her. We stopped talking about it in the end.

She still lived with her dad. She still does now, I think. She does nails for a living. I think she loves it, actually – she's always putting up these photos of all the nails she paints on Facebook. Big multicoloured talons. Stripes, spots, stars, little sprays of diamante jewels. Sometimes themed for St George's Day, Christmas, the Royal Wedding, whatever you like. She follows the soaps religiously. She has the odd boyfriend. I think she's seeing some guy at the moment who runs a bar. He sounds alright.

She doesn't seem angry. I don't think she's angry with me any more anyway. I don't know how she feels about Day. If you mention his name now, she just looks at you with this kind of determined blankness. She won't be drawn out. I've got no wish to draw her out, actually.

Did you draw her out, in the end?

I actually saw Day the last, out of the three of them, when I got back to England, I mean. He still lived up in Sale. He went to uni at Salford, which I always felt was a massive shame. *You could go anywhere you wanted,* I said to him at the time in one of my emails. *You've got the grades. More importantly, you've got the spark. Come to Oxford with me. You'll always regret it if you don't.*

Shut up, you elitist fanny, he wrote back.

He teaches English, now, in a secondary school. He likes it. He's good at it. I just… I don't know, I think he could do more. But it's not important.

Anyway, I wrote to him as soon as I got to Oxford, saying, *When can I come and see you?* He said he was busy, had stuff going on, for weeks. I was so impatient. Eventually I said, *Right, I'm coming on Saturday.* I don't remember the date, but it was near Christmas.

When I saw him, he was… different. Of course he was different, it had been years. He was a real man, with a bit of a beard and a few earrings and a flat. He'll have told you about the flat I suppose? Ah. Well, I'll leave that to him. We met for drinks, and we got drunk and held hands and talked for about eight hours, and then at the end of the night we went and slept together for the first time. And we've been together ever since. He had his own life by that point, was seeing somebody else at that time, but I, well, I didn't give him much choice about it. I wouldn't leave him alone. I wasn't going to let him go again.

It's not a simple relationship. It's… complicated. He's selfish, and cowardly, and deeply deeply annoying. He is, in many ways, frozen in time, back at the age of fourteen. The things that lots of us have gone through since then, that have sandpapered our corners down, made us normal… they somehow haven't done the same for him. He can't… he won't… you can't tell him what to do. So there are others. All the time. I know about them, I'm not kept in the dark. We're honest with each other.

Sometimes when we lie there in bed spooning, tucked into the pockets of one another, I am seized with wonder and rage that he would do this with another person, and I want to ask and reproach and whine. And then I regain control of myself, and I remind myself that I know him, that this is what I chose. And I kiss his arm or turn to kiss his face, and I stay quiet. I play the long game.

There have been times – when I've been angry with him – when I've gone off with somebody else for a while, and fawned all over them and let them believe I loved them. Tried it on like a new kind of shoe or something. Like, *Oh, so this is what a normal relationship feels like.* But it was… it never worked. I could never love anyone else. Not like that. Back then, that summer, I gave something away to Day that I can never get back. So now it's not mine to give to anyone else.

It's worth it, you know.

I believe in love. I believe in messy, hurtful, all-consuming love, that makes right and wrong seem like words that you only use to children. It's the only kind.

None of us are children any more, *Father.* Some of us never were.

Day

She's stronger than I am. You'll have worked that out by now.

We talked about the whole thing, of course. In the days following my release, before the start of the new school year. Before she moved away. We put our stories together, and from our pooled offerings of chance words and glances and observations, we managed to put together *our* version of what we think happened. We were able to be completely honest with each other about the nastier parts we played in the whole tragic farce, which is, in itself, a wonderful thing.

You probably don't like her very much now, I suppose?

I beg to differ. I think she is magnificent.

It's not as if we don't have disagreements, of course. I mean now, these days. Since we picked things up again. She's always trying to get me to move to London with her, for one thing. She's fallen into that repugnant post-Oxbridge trap of thinking that London's the only place in the world, and not being able to understand why anyone could possibly want to be anywhere else. I think often that she must be surprised, every time she gets on the train, to recollect there's a whole country up here. A whole multiplicity of real people with real lives who aren't Londoners. It's probably good for her.

I don't want to leave here, though. Like I told you at the beginning, I tried that, once. It wasn't right, it didn't work. Something draws me back here. To the place where it all happened. She can't understand that. She wants to draw a line under it all. She can't understand why that might not be what I want.

Sometimes I think too… she wants to keep me close. Control me, a bit. Keep an eye on me. I mean, don't misunderstand me, she's… I know I'm not easy to put up with, and I would never find… I don't know. There are times when I wish I didn't work the way I do. But I can only give her what there is of me. If she makes me unhappy, I'll leave her.

I still live on Chesterton Close, although the flats where I used to live have now been knocked down and replaced with some posh private ones I wouldn't stand a hope in hell of affording. D'you know where I live now? I live in Rachel's old house. Really, I do. But it's been sort of converted into four studio flats. I have one upstairs. What used to be her old bedroom.

Every time she comes to visit me, she comes in with her suit and shiny hair and expensive shoes, and looks around and says, *Weird*. Then she kicks them off, the shoes I mean, and lies down with me on the bed, and we forget ourselves a little. In my mind, to an extent, we become the teenagers we might have been if.

If it hadn't been for the keys.

Or the beauty of 5am.

And so it starts again.

This conversion thing. The process of building flats. Making houses into flats. It feels like everything's being broken down these days, into smaller and smaller pieces, doesn't it? I like it, myself. You used to walk down the street and look at a house, and know that it used to be one entity. One residence for one family. You knew what you were getting. Now, these days, you look at the façade of such a house, and you don't know. You've no idea how many homes might co-exist in there. How many people might be buried away in their own little cells, behind the same solid front.

D'you know what I mean?

Acknowledgments

I was enabled to publish this book by a competition run by Route Publishing. I would like to thank Route for their determination to find and help young authors in an industry that is notoriously hard to crack, and also to thank Arts Council England for supporting them in this aim. Victoria Price, Stephen May and Jodie Daber provided valuable assistance with the selection process, and David Peace was very generous in helping with publicity. I owe particular thanks to Ian Daley for his meticulous reading of my manuscript and helpful suggestions; to Isabel Galan for her energetic promotion of the novel; and to Rebecca Pedley for her insightful comments.

I am grateful to Fiona Tansey for telling me about police procedure, Edwin Kilby for his advice on arcane legislation, and Joe Dickinson for sharing his medical knowledge. Tram-Anh Doan has been extraordinarily generous with her professional advice and encouragement.

Rosa Dickinson, Amber Hammill, Harry Lee and Ryan Hanley read the first draft of my manuscript, and provided me with detailed, creative and encouraging feedback to a ludicrously tight schedule. They can expect to be pestered again for future projects; shoddy recompense for their generosity, perhaps, but also a sure sign of how highly I value their opinions.

My greatest debts are to Harry, who for three years bullied me to pick my pen back up and start doing the things I love again; and to my incredible parents Gilles and Noella, without whose unfailing support and encouragement I would never have started scribbling in the first place.

Sophie Coulombeau was brought up in Manchester. She studied at Trinity College, Oxford and the University of Pennsylvania and subsequently worked for the British Civil Service in London and the European Commission in Brussels. She is currently reading for a doctorate in English Literature at the University of York. *Rites* is her first novel.

For further information on this book,
and for Route's full book programme
please visit:

www.route-online.com